# The ROYALS

## Covet Me

### GENEVA LEE

ALSO BY GENEVA LEE

THE ROYALS SAGA

Command Me

Conquer Me

Crown Me

Crave Me

Covet Me

Capture Me

Complete Me


GOOD GIRLS DON'T

Catching Liam

Unwrapping Liam

Teaching Roman

Reaching Gavin


STANDALONE

The Sins That Bind Us

Two Week Turnaround

# The ROYALS

## Covet Me

### GENEVA LEE

evenafter
ROMANCE

Ever After Romance

www.EverAfterRomance.com

www.GenevaLee.com

First published, 2015. Second edition.

Print ISBN: 9781635765328

Cover Design © Date Book Designs. Image © iktash/Bigstockphoto.com. Image © marylia/Bigstockphoto.com

*For the girls who never lose hope...*

# CHAPTER ONE

*I*t finally happened. After weeks of tireless searching, I was here. I hadn't expected much from outside the building, but inside I'd discovered more than four walls and some windows. The studio was airy, and despite the chill that had crept through London as autumn moved ever closer to winter, a warm light flooded through the room highlighting all the space had to offer. I had found my own little corner of London, tucked snugly in Chelsea. This was where I would take the next step in my life.

Of course, everything from the walls to the shelves lining them needed a fresh coat of white paint. Maybe ivory. I also had a fair bit of furniture to obtain, given the space was entirely empty. But none of that bothered me. It had potential–and the right price tag.

"What do you think?" Julian, my inhumanly patient realtor, asked. I'd been a challenge for a man who normally sold business fronts to multi-billion dollar corporations.

But he had been a saint, showing me half of the available commercial properties in Central London, and his persistence had paid off.

"It's perfect," I murmured, my mind already imagining where office tables and garment racks would fit.

"The owner will want a twelve month term," he began to rattle off the particulars but none of it mattered. This was where the next phase of my life started. My fledgling idea was quickly becoming a real business: Bless. In a few months I'd have the space packed with desks and dresses. It all felt like a surreal dream.

An incoming call startled me from my fantasy, the familiar ringtone a reminder that I already had more than most women would dream of. I shot Julian an apologetic smile as I dug it out, but he waved it, having grown use to these interruptions in the last week.

"Hey, beautiful." Smith's gravelly voice sent goosebumps rippling over my skin. If any man could bring me to orgasm with words alone, it was this man. Thank god, I'd never told him that or he'd call me on the hour.

It was bad enough that just hearing him resulted in soaked panties. Then again that might have been the result of a week without physical contact. After he'd fired me as his personal assistant, we hadn't risked seeing each other more than a few times a week at first. It had been seven days—our longest successful streak at keeping our hands off each other—as of this morning. Judging from my body's reaction, it was time to break that record.

"I found it," I whispered into the phone. I didn't need to say more than that. Despite the distance we'd kept with one another for the past few weeks, I had no doubt he'd been keeping tabs on me. Still I couldn't tell him more. There was no reason to believe my new private line had been compromised, but there was also no reason to assume it hadn't. "Bless has a home."

"We should celebrate." The suggestiveness in his tone was far from subtle, and I hooked my one leg behind the other to soothe the ache growing rapidly between my thighs.

"Oh yeah?" As usual, he'd reduced me to simple sentences. When it came to Smith Price, I preferred to let him make the plans for both of us because his plans usually resulted in hours of agonizing, glorious, wild sex. I had a million things to worry about at the moment, but pleasure wasn't one of them. Not tonight, at least.

"Somewhere private—just the two of us. I'll text you the address."

"Yes, Sir," I breathed, not caring that Julian could overhear the conversation. My words were as much a promise of what tonight would bring as his invitation had been.

The line went dead and I was brought back to earth. Turning, I caught a knowing smirk on Julian's face as he checked his mobile.

"Whoever your mystery man is, I want to meet him." Julian slid the phone back in his breast pocket.

I raised an eyebrow and shook my head. "Why? So you can steal him?"

"Maybe we can share," he suggested in a teasing tone.

"This is one toy I definitely don't share." It came out more defensive than I'd intended, but I couldn't be blamed for my reaction. Smith was mine, and coping with our precarious situation had only made me more possessive of him.

Julian waved a pedicured hand. "As long as he feels the same way. "

Of that, I had no doubt.

"Let's go back to the office and start the paperwork," he said, switching topics.

Now that was something I could be talked into.

THE ADDRESS SMITH had sent me gave me no idea what to expect but when I arrived on a cozy, quiet street in Holland Park, I was a bit surprised. I'd anticipated a hotel not something so *residential*. A quick peek at my phone revealed that I was definitely in the right place. Grabbing my bag from the passenger seat, I slid out of the Mercedes, locking it twice despite the quaint neighborhood. The car, an overly lavish gift from my boyfriend, had become a second home over the last few weeks. I loved it almost as much as I loved the man who gave it to me.

I froze in my tracks, overwhelmed by the peculiar sensation that overcame me as I considered the fact that I loved him. Our relationship had endured its fair share of bumps in its short history already, and I couldn't quite be certain that love wasn't going to be a major road block. Neither of us had said it. It had been implied, and perhaps I was being stubborn but I wasn't going to be the first one to pop the l-word.

Maybe I was simply scared. Smith was still a mystery to me in so many ways, and the last man I'd thought I'd loved had proven my judgment wasn't the best when it came to men.

But Smith Price wasn't any man. He was something more—something primal and commanding. He stole my breath away and decided when I could have it back.

*Get a handle on yourself!* Shouldering my purse, I shook off my apprehension, writing it off as cold feet. It had been nearly two weeks since I'd seen him. That was enough to make any woman doubt herself, but I wasn't that girl. Not anymore.

Still I gripped the railing a little too tightly as I climbed the steps to the house. The night air brushed across my naked sex, reminding me exactly why I was here. My panties, per Smith's preference, had come off in the car and been shoved into my bag. I felt exposed and powerful at the same time. Things might be strained between us but I had exactly what he wanted.

Before I reached the top step, the door swung open, revealing *exactly what I wanted*. My knees buckled slightly at I drank in Smith in his charcoal, grey three piece suit. It was unjustifiable that the sight of any human being could have such an effect of me. I'd be lucky to make it inside before I was on my knees in front of him.

Smith's handsome face was blank as he welcomed me in, but I spotted the amused glint in his green eyes and the slight twitch of his lips that proved he was holding back a smile. I'd fallen for that cocky smirk as hard as I'd fallen for him. It had been my undoing when we met. Now knowing it was there, hiding behind his calculated stare, made me wet.

"Hello, beautiful." He took my bag and threw it on the ground, not waiting for my greeting before he'd scooped me up and carried me past the foyer. My arms coiled around his neck, inviting his lips to find mine. But he had more self-control than I did. His mouth pressed to my forehead before he deposited me on a leather sofa.

"Like it?" he asked.

I blinked, momentarily dazzled by his presence, and forced myself to look around the cozy room. Paintings that clearly fell into the priceless category hung along the walls and a fire crackled in the ornate fireplace. It looked much more like his law office than his own home, and I shot him a questioning look as I replied, "I do."

"One of my investments," he explained as he unbuttoned his jacket. He didn't take it off, which pleased me. I had plans for him tonight that included that suit.

I was so absorbed in my own fantasies that it took me a minute to realize he'd said something else. "Sorry?"

Smith's head cocked to the side, and he sighed as he ran a hand over his head, ruffling his dark blond hair. "I can see that you need a little pleasure before business."

"*Yes, Sir.*"

The simple statement ignited a fire in his eyes that burned so fiercely that I bit down on my lip to keep from moaning. I'd given him the nickname in a moment of petulance. It had stuck when I discovered how demanding he was behind closed doors—and how eager I was to please him.

Smith leaned down, placing his palms on the arm of the sofa as he shook his head. "We play by my rules. Do you need a reminder?"

That sounded very much like a threat and a promise all rolled into one. He'd been known to dish out a playful spanking when I teased him or played coy, but I'd yet to bear the full brunt of what I knew he was capable of delivering. The thought might have scared me before, but as the days passed without his hands on my body, I found myself desperate for his touch.

"You want it that bad, huh?" he said, employing his uncanny knack for guessing exactly what was on my mind. "Don't try to force my hand, Belle, or I'll make you wait for a punishment even longer than I'll make you wait for an orgasm."

I glowered back at him, unwilling to show that his warning had deflated me. Instead I pushed myself up and crossed my legs, taking care that he got a glimpse of what I *wasn't* wearing under my skirt. "So you bought this place?"

"A few years ago." He made no sign that he'd noticed my lack of underwear. Disappointing. "I meant to sell it."

"Didn't get around to it?" I asked dryly. Only Smith was capable of sitting on a prime piece of London real estate for so long without making a move. Another symptom of his maddening self-control. His bank account allowed for it, while the rest of us were stuck sharing flats.

"I have other ideas now." But he didn't elaborate further. His eyes cooled as his thoughts went elsewhere.

I took a deep breath and waited for him to return to me. When he didn't, I took a chance. "I missed you."

It was a simple statement, but emotion colored my voice. Instantly, I wished I could take it back. I'd promised him I could be strong when he'd revealed the precarious nature of our situation. Melancholy sentiments had no place in our arrangement. For the most part, I'd been too busy focusing on my sudden entrepreneurial reality to worry about our relationship. At least in the waking hours. It was harder when I finally dragged myself to my bed— alone. Now that he was in front of me, the ache that had occupied those restless nights was swiftly overtaking my resolution.

But instead of reprimanding me, he sank down beside me and pulled me onto his lap. "Beautiful."

His pet name for me calmed the longing that had suddenly swept through my body. Although it didn't entirely soothe me.

"I spent all afternoon planning what I am going to do to you," he murmured as his index finger tipped my chin up to meet his gaze.

"And?" I prompted hopefully.

His mouth twisted as he winked. "I think you'll approve. But I thought we could talk for a bit. I'm told normal couples discuss their day before they get naked."

*Couple.* It seemed like too casual a term for the bond he and I had already formed. And normal? That definitely didn't apply to us. Still, there was a certain appeal to the concept.

"Normal couples don't have to sneak around," I reminded him. So much for trying things his way.

"Normal couples," he responded tightly, "don't have homicidal bosses."

There was that. Our separation hadn't been by choice, a fact that I wished I could forget. Smith's ties to his employer were far from average. He was caught in a tangled web of treachery that I'd only narrowly avoided being trapped in myself. Thanks to him, there had been no sign that Hammond, the man pulling the strings that kept Smith tethered to the past, had any further interest in me. That would change if he knew things weren't over between the two of us.

"Tell me about Bless," he commanded, obviously ready for a change in topic.

There was so much to tell him, even though so little had actually been accomplished. "I found a studio in Chelsea within my budget."

"Budget shouldn't be in your vocabulary." His forehead creased as he spoke, but I cut him off before he could force me to take more money.

"I'm starting a business. Of course, I need to consider my finances, and besides that, it's exactly what I was looking for. If it had been too much I would have told you," I lied. I had absolutely no intention of taking any more of his funds without actually needing them.

"What's mine is yours."

"Is that so?" I asked playfully, toying with his belt buckle. It was increasingly clear to me that we both needed to loosen up, and I had a pretty good idea of how we could to that.

9

My response earned me my first genuine smile. "Are we calling it quits on the small talk?"

"We could chat about the weather, but honestly, you aren't the only one with plans tonight."

"Think you're going to top me, beautiful?" He ran a finger across my lower lip and my mouth opened instinctively.

Now that would be impossible, especially given how much I craved his authority. I pressed my thighs tightly together, afraid to leave a damp spot on his wool trousers. "I wouldn't dream of it."

"Good girl." I felt his fingers close over my skirt. Pulling it down, he wrenched the garment off and tossed it away. "I was going to suggest we have a bite to eat, but there's only one thing I want for dinner."

So much for protecting his suit pants. I bit my lower lip, spreading my legs in welcome.

"I want to see the whole menu first," he whispered into my ear as he unbuttoned my blouse with the slow attention to detail that drove me crazy. His fingertips grazed slowly over each section of newly exposed skin. Then they skimmed across the lace cups of my bra before he unhooked it. It fell away, and in one fluid motion, he lifted me into his arms and stood. "I think you'll find the upper floor much more interesting."

He nibbled at my neck as we ascended the staircase. By the time we reached the bedroom, I was breathless with anticipation. Smith deposited me onto the bed and took a step back, surveying his prize as he began to undress. He took his time with this as well. Smith was the type of man who might push a woman against a wall, shove her panties aside, and fuck her, fully clothed. But when he took a woman to bed—when he took me to bed—that urgency was replaced by a deliberation that sent shivers across my skin.

Shrugging off his jacket, he folded it in half and laid it over a chair in the corner. He repeated the action with his tie, then his shirt. Each garment given the utmost care. It was the world's slowest—and sexiest—striptease. Because Smith didn't reserve that treatment for his expensive suits alone. Every inch of my body would be shown the same attention.

Besides, when his shorts dropped to the floor I got my first glimpse of what was on my menu, and god, I wanted a taste. Scrambling onto my hands and knees, I crawled to the foot of the bed, mouth open. Smith prowled forward, the curves and ridges of his muscular body haloed in moonlight. He stopped a foot short of me, giving me a closer look at what I wanted while keeping it out of reach.

"Ask."

My whole body was asking, but that wasn't what he meant. At first I'd found Smith's dominant nature intimidating. Now I found it liberating, and after the week I'd had, I wanted nothing more than to lose myself entirely to his domination. "Please, Sir."

"Roll over," he instructed as he came closer.

I turned onto my back, instinctively hanging my head over the edge of the bed so that he could guide the crown of his cock to my lips.

"Have you been touching yourself?"

I did my best to shake my head 'no' but I was way too focused on wrapping my mouth around his luscious organ.

"But you wanted to," he guessed. He paused to groan as I swallowed his shaft. "I know how hungry your pussy is. It's almost as insatiable as your greedy little mouth. It must have been hard to deny your needs, beautiful. You may touch yourself now."

Reaching back, I gripped his root for leverage, my free hand delving willingly between my folds. Nothing got me hotter than being on display for him, except maybe being splayed out under his possessive eyes with his dick in my mouth. My body trembled when my fingertip found my swollen clit. I circled it, rolling my hips against the welcome pressure. Truthfully, I had no desire to touch myself when I was apart from him, knowing it could never satisfy my craving. Only he could do that.

"Fuck me, beautiful. Your mouth feels good," Smith rasped, his eyes hooded as he watched me.

God, I loved putting on a show for him. Nothing had ever made me feel more alive—more irresistible—than when those eyes were on me. I existed for these moments.

He pulled away from me and leaned down so that his face was inches from mine. His arm snaked down, gripping my wrist and bringing my arousal-coated fingers to his lips. "I need to taste that."

Smith sucked each finger leisurely, turning the pulse at my core into a sharp, insistent stab of want. My legs dropped open on the bed as I began to squirm, restraining myself from pulling him down on top of me. He dropped his hold on my hand, his mouth still clamped over my middle finger, and hooked his arms under my shoulders. Finally releasing me, he flipped me onto my stomach and climbed into the bed. I didn't dare move as he positioned himself behind me. I knew better than to interrupt him when he was taking the reins. His hands dug into my hips as he wrenched my spread thighs over his lap. I was face-down on the mattress, my hands clenching the linens for strength.

"I've missed this." He stroked his palm across my buttocks and down to the quivering mound between my legs, sending a jolt of electricity charging through the sensitive spot. "I can feel how much you want to be spanked. Did you miss my palm on your ass?"

"Yes, Sir," I moaned against the fabric. And I had. It made me feel filthy how much I'd missed it. The first slap hit the right cheek lightly, and I bit down on the comforter, afraid I would come just from the contact. Heat blossomed across the tender skin, and Smith caressed it lovingly.

"More?" he prompted.

I nodded, my teeth still clenched.

"Ask me for what you want."

My mouth fell open, the plea falling wantonly from my lips. "Please spank me."

"Happily."

The next thwack was harder, jarring me so forcefully my legs tried to clamp shut against Smith's waist. I just needed a little friction. But Smith was far too skilled to allow that. Instead I endured a series of smacks ranging from playful to punishing. When he finally stopped, my ass stung from the erotic assault. My mind was blank, capable only of processing the hot, pulsating sensation spreading through my behind. Smith didn't say anything as he yanked my body another few inches back and inserted his cock inch-by-glorious-inch in my throbbing entrance. His hands stayed on my waist, keeping me still as my body acclimated to his girth.

"You're so wet and so tight. Are you ready to come for me?"

I choked out a yes. *Oh God, yes. Yes. Yes. Yes.* It was the only word that held any meaning, and I screamed it as he thrust inside me, liberating the climax that he'd built in my core. He hammered relentlessly so that with each violent stroke another wave of pleasure seized hold of me. I clawed at the bed, trying to hold on to the feeling. I never wanted it to stop. I never wanted him to free me. But as the spasms quieted, he withdrew and guided me carefully onto my back before pushing back inside.

"Look at me," he demanded in a gruff voice. "I want you to see what you do to me, Belle."

I forced my drooping eyes open as he rocked slowly. Smith's thumb found my clit, and I watched as his shaft disappeared inside my body.

It was the hottest thing I'd ever seen. Smith towering between my spread legs, the root of his shaft visible between the pink folds of my flesh.

My muscles tensed, already readying themselves for the next unstoppable onslaught.

"Fuck, beautiful!" he grunted as I felt the first unmistakable jet shoot against my velvet channel.

I lost myself with him, my legs wrapping around his

waist to urge him faster as we unraveled together. When he finally stilled, he gathered me in his arms, sealing his mouth over mine. Our limbs tangled together as the kiss deepened. This was where I belonged. This was the man I belonged to. Breaking apart, we collapsed, still knit around each other. His hand cupped the side of my face, drawing me back to his lips and the promise of much more to come.

# CHAPTER TWO

$\mathcal{D}$espite the crowd at CoCo's the next afternoon, I felt more relaxed than ever. It was amazing what a night of orgasmic bliss could do for a girl. From the corner of the restaurant, Lola waved me over to the table, grinning widely. The smile vanished from her face as a waiter appeared at the table to take our drink orders. The lanky server looked a bit too pleased to have two women in his section. He squatted beside the table, but before he could get a word out, Lola cut him off.

"Bourbons. West's please," she instructed him, dismissing him without a second glance in his direction. When he disappeared toward the bar, she shot me an annoyed look. "He's been hovering like a puppy since I sat down."

"That bad?" I asked with a laugh as I hooked my bag over the back of my chair.

"Worse. He needs to reconsider his tactics if he thinks he's going to be picking up more than my signed bill." Lola shrugged good-naturedly and tapped her phone on, switching to business mode. "Now let's chat about where you're at with publicity."

One of the reasons I'd approached Lola to tackle this issue was due to her ability to get down to business. Today was obviously going to be no exception. The trouble was that I didn't really know where to start. Unfolding my napkin and placing it on my lap to buy time, I tried to think. "Honestly, I just secured a business front. I still haven't received the logo comps and we haven't begun to buy inventory yet."

Not to mention the fact that most of my ideas were mere scribbles in a notebook at this phase.

"Have you written a business plan?" she asked as she swiftly typed a note on her mobile.

"Um, not exactly. Not an official one. I have a lot of notes." Smith had pushed me on this as well, but he'd also been more than happy to distract me from completing the task.

"That's your second order of business then. Before you jump into it, I need a one page summary pitching the idea and explaining the subscription tiers and how much you anticipate charging."

I raised an eyebrow at her. "I thought you were consulting."

Lola tilted her head. In this thoughtful position, she looked more like her sister, Clara, than usual. "About that..."

I braced myself as she paused. If she backed out now, I was screwed. I barely had time to shower every day. There was no time to find another publicist willing to strategize this early in the game.

"I want in," she said, surprising me. "This is my last year at university. Next semester I need a job. Know anyone that might hire me?"

There was no ignoring the implication in her question. "You want to actually work for me?"

So far the reactions to my unexpected foray into business had been a mixed bag. Most of my friends were enthusiastic but only mildly interested. My mother had almost had a heart attack. And Smith? I still wasn't certain. He'd fronted the expenses, but he'd also been looking for a way to get me out of Hammond's sights. Funding my company might have simply been a calculated move.

"Unless you don't want me." Lola took a sip of water, her expression totally unreadable.

"No!" I said too loudly, cringing when a few other patrons turned to stare at me. I lowered my voice and leaned over the table. "I definitely want you. I think I've got the right idea for the business side of things, but I'm not a PR expert. It's just...I can't really pay you. *Yet.*"

*Or maybe ever.* I silenced the voice. It was too early to give up.

"I figured." Her response was nonchalant. She tucked a dark strand of hair behind her ear. "Look, I don't really need money. What I do need is something I can get excited about. My father has been breathing down my neck to partner with him on some new start-up, but for many reasons, I don't want to go that direction. So since I don't have to worry about money, I want to build something of my own. I could even contribute additional finances."

"Finances aren't an issue," I reassured her as my cheeks heated.

"Then let's get started," she suggested as the waiter reappeared with the bourbons.

"We have a business name and a studio space, are we ready to get started?"

She smirked at this, running her finger along the rim of her glass. "We have an idea. Let's start selling it. I want to approach the high-end magazines by week's end to do features on you and the business. Publications create content months in advance. We'll want the press when we're up and running, not months after we launch."

Things were moving fast. A week ago I had an idea, now I had a partner, a storefront, and more on my plate than I'd bargained for. It was beyond exciting, but underneath the initial thrill, there was a fair amount of anxiety. "It's okay to be scared, right?"

"Yes. If your life doesn't scare you a little, you probably aren't living," she said without hesitation, raising her glass. "To partners."

"I hope you're right." I touched my drink to hers and shook my head. She had no idea how much my life scared me sometimes. "To terrifying new possibilities."


BY THE TIME we'd finished a short strategy meeting, I found myself anxious to get back to the office. The blissful calm that I'd experienced since leaving Smith this morning had been replaced by a frantic desire to focus. In two days, I'd managed to secure an office and a business partner. Digging my phone out, I bypassed checking my overrun inbox and tapped out a message to Edward.

BELLE: Bless has two things to celebrate this week!

EDWARD: I knew you could do it, babe! Drinks on Saturday? I want to hear all about it.

BELLE: You're on.

EDWARD: I'll text you the details in a few.

Before I could drop my mobile back into my purse, an incoming call buzzed from an unknown number. I stared at the screen, torn over answering. I knew I should let it go to voicemail given the circumstances, but I couldn't ignore the fact that I was a businesswoman now. The call could be important. In the end, curiosity won out over patience.

"Hello?" I answered.

"Have you reviewed the documents I messengered to your flat?"

My eyes closed involuntarily at the sound of my mother's voice. "Did you block your caller ID?"

"I can't get you to answer my calls, and those documents are of a time-sensitive nature," she said, sounding far from apologetic about deceiving me.

I'd been avoiding her calls for weeks, along with the unopened envelope that had arrived after our last disastrous visit. She'd made it clear then that I was nothing more than a signature to her.

"I also heard you're going through with this foolish website business," she continued swiftly. No doubt she had a lot of complaints to lodge before I ended the call. "Where did the capital for that come from? Did your aunt finance it?"

"Aunt Jane hasn't given me a penny." *Just emotional support, I added to myself.*

"It would have been a far wiser course of action to focus your energy on our estate."

My estate, the unwanted birthright I'd received when my father died, was the last thing I wanted to think about. Once I'd been willing to marry well to keep it afloat. Now I didn't care if it sank, or my mother along with it.

"I assume you have everything under control," I responded coolly. She'd never asked me for my opinion on how we might deal with the estate's debts. Instead she'd simply harassed me to find a way to maintain her aristocratic lifestyle.

"The producers want to start shooting the show this Christmas," she said, her tone taking on a level of exasperation somewhere between panic attack and meltdown.

"I'll review it when I have time." In truth, if it meant getting her off my back, I'd sign the entire grounds over to the BBC immediately. But I suspected it was going to be more complicated than that, and I didn't want to spend what little time I had with my personal legal counsel talking through contracts.

"I would hate to have to take further action," she threatened.

I stopped in my tracks, accidentally causing a couple to knock into me on the pavement. Mouthing an apology, I darted to the front of a shop. "Care to explain what that means?"

"If you have a company, you have assets," she said in a smooth voice. "The estate is in your name, which means I can transfer its debts to you."

"If you do that," I said between gritted teeth, "pack your bags."

"I can't believe you would throw the woman who gave birth to you out on the street!"

"That is one debt that's been paid, and I definitely don't owe you for anything else," I hissed, quickly adding, "I'll review the contracts."

I hung up, fury vibrating through me. Pressing my back to the glass window, I stared out at the midday crowds while I forced myself to breathe. Smith would never allow her to ruin Bless, but I couldn't ask him for help without coming clean about the depth of my estate's financial crisis. I'd sign the papers and with them grant her and it a few more years of life support until I could finally pull the plug on them both.

## CHAPTER THREE

*T*ugging at the bill of my baseball cap, I glanced casually down the street. I'd had worse ideas in my life but not many. But after my recent rendezvous with Belle, I found myself too distracted at work to accomplish much. Her recent absence felt more acute than it had in weeks, as though I'd opened a fresh wound and had to restart the healing process. Except I didn't want to. Instead, her absence festered and stung, leaving me desperate to claw at the itch.

I approved of her choice in location, her building situated in a quiet pocket of the neighborhood where she would be tucked away safely. Maybe it would help soothe the possessive curiosity that ate away at me all hours of the day. I knew where she lived. Now I needed to see where she worked. I'd reined in my desire to have her followed, settling instead for the satisfaction of knowing her car was LoJacked. Too much interference on my part would undermine the front we'd contrived. But it wasn't easy having my heart walking around outside my body.

The knob welcomed me in, a fact I noted with displeasure. She should be more careful. I opened the door and poked my head into the studio. She was at her desk, her usually neat hair piled into a sexy tangle on the top of her head. The loose black t-shirt she wore draped over her pert breasts. She'd never shown up in my office dressed this casually. I'd have remembered yanking her jeans around her ankles if she had. Her lack of makeup, save for her bright, crimson lipstick, only made her look sexier. This was Belle behind closed doors. This was Belle on a night in. This was the Belle I coveted—the natural, untamed version she hid under couture dresses and high heels. It was the part of her she kept to herself—the part I wanted to claim as my own.

"You should really lock this," I announced as I quietly entered.

She jumped, her hand fluttering to her chest, at the unexpected interruption. Confusion flashed in her pale blue eyes as she took in my similarly dressed down appearance before her sinful lips twisted into a wicked smile.

"Jeans and ball cap? Is it casual Friday?" she asked, dropping her pencil on the desk.

"Wednesday, but I took the afternoon off." I closed the door, making certain it locked behind me.

She leaned forward, affording me a better view down her shirt. "What's in the bag?"

If she wasn't more careful about putting her tits on

display, she'd never find out. "I brought my girlfriend lunch."

"You are committed to this normal bit," she said.

*I'm committed to you, beautiful.*

I kept the thought to myself, uncertain where it came from and what exactly it meant. Also because it sounded a bit too much like a fucking greeting card. I dropped to the floor and folded my legs underneath me. "Have you eaten?"

She shook her head and joined me as I pulled containers out and handed her one.

"What do you think?" she asked, waving her spoon at the space surrounding us before digging into her curry.

I looked closer, uninterested in eating myself. "Lots of potential."

"It's a blank space," she admitted.

But I understand what she saw in the studio. It was large enough to accommodate a start-up inventory. Eventually she would need a bigger home base for Bless, but for now it would keep her busy—a distraction I was counting on.

We discussed plans over chicken tikka masala, but I hardly noticed the food. All I could see was how her face lit up as she shared her vision for the empire she was creating. She'd come in to my life deceptively, a pawn in an agenda she knew little about. Now that I'd made her part of my life for real, I would do everything in my power to help her achieve her dreams.

"Care to give me the grand tour?" I asked when we'd piled the leftovers back in the sack. Standing, I held out my hand, drawing her up to her feet and into my arms.

"There's not much to show you." Her voice took on the breathless tone that always made me hard. "The loo's through that door. My desk is right here. That's all."

"Show me what it's going to be," I encouraged her, doing my best to ignore the steady throb of my cock.

Taking my hand, she led me over to the shelves. "This is where the packing and shipping materials will be. Over there"—she pointed to the adjacent wall—"we'll have the clothing racks. I'm still working out the best system for organizing them."

I glanced over at the rickety table she was using as her desk. "And that's where your desk will be."

"That's where my desk is." She frowned a little as she surveyed it.

I made a mental note to purchase one and have it delivered.

"You're plotting," she accused me. "I have everything I need and enough money to get a base inventory ordered. A desk isn't on the priority list."

"You need a new desk," I said dryly. "One for an executive."

"Are you insulting mine? It holds my computer. It's the right height. It's yet to fall apart." She continued to rattle off a list of all its benefits before I pressed my index finger to her mouth.

"Beautiful, there's one problem with it."

She narrowed her eyes and drew back. "Which is?"

"I can't fuck you on that one," I said in a gruff voice, grabbing her hips and yanking her back. Show and tell was over. "I've been dreaming about nailing this hot CEO on her power desk."

"I guess you'll have to settle for the floor."

I raised an eyebrow, taking her chin in my hand. "You don't belong on the floor...unless you're on your knees."

"I'll write that down." The slight tremble in her voice undermined her barb. It was my favorite form of foreplay, watching as she shifted from bold and confident to panting and desperate.

Trailing the back of my hand over her cheek, I murmured, "I'm so fucking proud of you."

"I haven't done anything yet," she whispered, an uncharacteristically shy edge running through her words.

"Don't do that," I ordered. "Don't doubt yourself, because there's nothing to doubt."

She tilted her face against my hand, her eyes closing. "I needed to hear that."

"I'm going to tell you every day," I promised her. I would find a way to, even if it was nothing more than a text. My business was built on the bones of my father. Everything about my life was the result of my own broken soul. Belle's career would never be that way. It would be honest and empowering and daring—just like her.

"I miss you," she said in a low voice that sliced through me.

"I know, beautiful." Cupping her jaw, I angled my mouth to meet hers and brushed a kiss over her lips. "This won't last forever."

"What if I want it to?" Her eyelashes fluttered down as she spoke.

"This separation won't last. We"—I corrected her—"are forever."

Christ. So much for not giving her too much hope. I shouldn't have told her that, not when I couldn't stand behind those words, even if I meant them.

"How can you be sure?" Her voice was so small, as fragile and lovely as she was.

She was asking a lot of me today, more than I was able to give her. I could only show her by sating her thirst for reassurance in a more primal language—one I knew she understood. Slipping my hands to her waist, I unzipped her jeans and dipped my hand into her panties. Holy fuck, she was soaked. I'd been correct. This was exactly the consolation she needed.

"Does it make you wet to know I own you?" I asked as my lips swept down her throat. "To know I've claimed you as mine?

"Forever?"

"Forever, beautiful," I repeated as I pushed her jeans to the floor. "You belong to me."

She watched transfixed as I freed my cock from my pants. I loved when she looked at me like that—apprehensive and fervent, as if it was the first time. Lifting her by the ass, I carried her to the wall. She wiggled in my arms, pushing her hot, moist pussy in invitation against my shaft. It slid slickly across my tip and my restraint slipped. I slammed her against the plaster, sending dust scattering over our heads.

"Is that what you need?" I asked, grinding against her swollen mound. She shuddered as she nodded, bucking furiously in a frantic ploy for more contact. Her fingers gripped my shirt as she urged me closer, her shapely legs coiling around my waist. "This is why I have to tie you up, beautiful. You can't fucking control yourself, can you?"

She bit her lip, but it didn't hide her smirk. The woman could give as good as she got. She knew exactly what buttons to push.

"You want to play coy?" I rolled my groin, so that she couldn't get enough leverage. Pinning her with my hips, I wrenched her arms over her head and continued to circle her engorged clit mercilessly until I could feel it throbbing against the head of my dick.

"Bad girls have to wait for it," I warned as I bit her collarbone. Bending lower, I captured the peak of her breast in my teeth and began to suck the tip through the soft cotton of her t-shirt. She arched against me, fighting my hold on her wrists, but I held her steady. "Bad girls need to be taught lessons like *patience.*"

A low, throaty cry escaped her mouth as I moved on to her next tit. My dick jolted at the sound, growing so hard that it physically hurt. Fuck, that was the cost of patience. I was starving for her, turning inside out with want. I wanted to push inside her sweet cunt and destroy her like she threatened to destroy my self-control. But if it meant I could torture this beautiful, perfect woman until she was begging for release, I could subsist on her squeals and moans. Each sound she made was more delicious than the last.

"Please," she sobbed. Dropping her lips, she continued

to plead, but her whispered entreaties were lost on me. This was becoming a lesson in temperance for both of us.

"*Shh*, beautiful. I'm going to make you come—*hard*— when I'm ready for you to."

I was always ready for her to come, but this time I needed to watch—needed to see my dick marking what was mine. Dropping her hands, I guided her back to her feet as she scrabbled at the wall so as not to fall. Her shirt clung to her belly, giving me a better view of her soft, creamy thighs pressed together so tightly that only the barest hint of her delicate pink folds was visible. Quivering. Raw. It was fucked up to get off on making her wait and I gave not one fuck. Gripping her hip, I spun her around and pushed her gently to the wall. Belle melted into it, arms splayed, sticking her ass out to me like an offering.

I hooked my arm under her left leg and pinned her knee against the plaster. I shoved inside her, giving her no time to acclimate as I began to drive my cock deep, the force of my thrusts lifting her entirely off her other foot.

"Oh God, I'm yours," she cried out. "Yours."

"Yes, you are," I crooned, my hand sliding from her hip to clutch her neck. I buried my mouth against her ear, relishing her soft gasps as I squeezed. "I'm going to fuck your pussy raw so that you remember that."

She tensed around me, clamping down in quick, violent surges— and then she fell away, coming with such force that the pulse of her channel milked my own climax from me. I stayed inside her watching as my climax leaked around my root, our bodies still notched together. When I finally withdrew, it spilled down her seam and she dashed toward the loo to clean up.

I tucked my dick back in my pants. Satisfied but not altogether sated. She reappeared, darting around me to reach her pants, but I snagged them before she could. My mind already preoccupied with the other spots in her office that needed to be christened.

"I won't get any work done today without those." She planted her hands on her narrow hips.

"Consider it repayment for all the times you kept me distracted at the office." I dangled them just out of reach.

"You hired me...and fired me."

"And now I have a perpetual erection at work," I admitted. "Maybe I should come and work for you. Of course, my office has much sturdier furniture."

She licked her lips, no doubt remembering the things I'd done to her on my desk.

I smirked and tossed her the pants. "That's why you need a real desk."

# CHAPTER FOUR

"What does it mean that we've chosen a quiet little spot for Saturday night drinks?" I asked as I slid onto the stool beside Edward's. The pub he'd chosen was off the beaten path, far away from the usual hot spots we frequented on the weekends. Apart from a few regulars who took up residence at their tables as if they were holding court, the place was empty. After the busy week I'd had, I was more than happy with his choice.

"I suppose that we're in danger of becoming adults." He pecked my cheek in welcome and grabbed my hands to study my ensemble. "You even look like an adult."

I batted his hand away as I adjusted the skirt of my dress underneath me. Since he'd texted me to meet him here, I'd opted for a simple navy sheath, leather jacket and boots. "Are you saying you don't approve? Because you're wearing jeans. I didn't even know you owned jeans."

"No. Only that we are in danger of being old," he teased,

a bemused grin lighting across his boyish face. "I suppose our dancing days are behind us."

"Next stop the retirement village, but first a drink."

Edward passed me a pint with a laugh. I took the beer, clinking it against his.

"So I was told we needed to celebrate," he prompted.

I quickly filled him in on the developments of the last week. Edward played the best friend perfectly, exclaiming gleefully at the right moments.

"And how are you feeling about all of this?" he asked.

Edward had kept his questions to a minimum since I had surprised him and Clara with the news that I was starting my own business. If he had any concerns over where my capital was coming from, he hadn't expressed them. He also hadn't questioned my sanity. He'd left that part to me.

"Overwhelmed," I admitted, "but in a good way."

It was nice to talk about it with someone who didn't want to bounce strategy ideas. One of the reasons I'd left Lola off the invitation list for the evening. And while Smith was certainly interested, we both had a tendency to get easily distracted by other activities.

"Well, if you need any dashing models, I am available." He struck a ridiculous pose that sent us both into a fit of giggles.

"Sadly, we're focusing entirely on female lines at the moment."

"My offer stands," he said in a serious tone.

Swatting him on the shoulder, I decided it was time to change the subject. "So wedding bells?"

"My reprieve was short." He downed the rest of his drink and shook his head. "I'm afraid you can leave the betting pool open. We haven't set a date."

"You can't avoid it forever." I'd seen how massive his fiance David's wedding planning notebook had gotten in the last few weeks. Edward was working on borrowed time.

"Soon," he promised.

"Ugh, I hate when men do that!" I snapped. "And I bet David does as well."

"Why would you say that?" he countered, motioning for another round from the bartender. "Are you having romantic troubles?"

"Don't try to turn this around on me," I warned him.

"All's fair. You've been avoiding the subject nearly as long as I've been avoiding the aisle."

"That's not even remotely true," I said flatly. "I got fired a few weeks ago. How long have you been engaged?"

"Nope," he stopped me. "I changed the subject. You got fired, but have you ceased all duties involving Smith Price?"

"God, no wonder you're avoiding the altar if you think of it as a duty!"

"I knew it!" he exclaimed, shaking a finger in my direction. "Did he fire you because he couldn't get any work done around you?"

The arrival of the next round saved me from having to answer the question. It wasn't that I wanted to keep things from Edward, but the status of my relationship needed to remain on the hush-hush.

"You know I could really use a second set of eyes on these logos I just got."

"You really are all business." Edward bumped my shoulder. "Show them to me."

"I guess Lola isn't the only workaholic." But even as I spoke, I pulled my phone from my jacket pocket.

If Edward had an opinion on that, he didn't say anything. He had plenty of thoughts on the logo, however. An hour later, we'd settled on combining the modern style of one with the graphic of another.

"It's perfect," I said, visualizing what the revised logo was going to look like as a text flashed across the top of my mobile. Tapping it, I read through Smith's message twice. It didn't make any sense, but before I could respond, another one appeared. There was no mistaking the picture attached. I recognized the lush velvet corridor immediately.

He wanted me to meet at Velvet. The club he'd sold. The place he'd asked me to stay away from.

I swallowed hard, trying to digest his request as I checked to make sure the message was actually from him. It had come from his number. He had to have a good reason for inviting me, but everything about it felt wrong. A flutter of panic tumbled through my belly as I considered what it would be like to walk back through that door.

"What's wrong?" Edward said, studying my face.

"Nothing." I forced myself to sound cheerful as I pocketed my mobile. "Apparently I have a date."

"David will be thrilled to have me home early. He got the new issue of*Modern Wedding*."

I tried to smile, but my mouth had stopped working; instead my heart raced as we said our goodbyes. When I finally slid into the Mercedes, I pulled my mobile back out, praying I would find another message informing me that this was all some ill-conceived joke. But there was nothing waiting for me, which meant if I wanted answers, there was only one place to go. Buckling up, I braced myself for the ride ahead.

# CHAPTER FIVE

"*I* thought I was the one with the twisted sense of humor," Georgia said as she entered her office and found me staring at the security feed for Velvet's outer door.

"There's nothing funny about this." I didn't take my eyes from the screen. Part of me still hoped Belle would make another choice. But she hadn't called me. She hadn't questioned my message. And that meant she was on her way.

"What exactly is your plan?" Georgia asked. "I know she hates this place, but I've seen it in her big doe eyes. She likes it rough. What if she shows up expecting you to tie her up?"

"Belle has no interest in anything this place has to offer." She'd made that clear after her first—and only—visit here. It was a sentiment we shared. The only thing I found more sickening than finding myself back inside the club was knowing that I had lured Belle here as well.

Georgia moved next to me, adjusting the ties of her revealing corset and leaving me eye level with her exposed tits. "If you aren't willing to give her a good whipping, I would be happy to."

She fingered the petite cat-o-nine tails sitting on her desk for emphasis.

"No one touches her," I growled.

"You're adorable when you're acting like a caveman." Georgia smirked and picked up the whip. "Need to let out some of that pent-up hostility?"

We hadn't scened together in years. It disgusted me now to recall how far she pushed me to go each time. Georgia wasn't truly happy until she was nearly broken. With most people she put on a brave face. She'd only ever begged me to hurt her more. Between that and the absolute lack of sexual chemistry between us, it had always been a one-sided experience.

Hammond had ruined my life, but he'd twisted her into a creature incapable of feeling anything outside of pain.

"I'm not interested." I pushed the proffered whip away.

Her coy grin vanished into haughtiness. She could see that I pitied her.

"Submission isn't about sex," she spit out at me. "Or have you forgotten that?"

I hadn't. I knew exactly how it worked. "I'm not in the lifestyle, Georgia. Not anymore."

"Bloody hell, you aren't," she challenged me. "I saw how she watched the members the night she came here. You've collared her."

"You can't collar Belle." The idea was laughable.

Collaring a submissive and leashing a wanton woman were two very different things. Belle responded to kink. She welcomed it, but that went no further than sex—for either of us.

"Well, aren't you the enlightened, sensitive male." Georgia screwed her delicate features into a grimace.

It didn't matter what she thought. The truth was that it would be much easier if I could count on Belle to be obedient, but I didn't want her that way. Yes, I wanted to collar her and tie her up and fuck her until she couldn't walk. But in the morning I wanted to hear everything that came out of her smart, sexy mouth.

"That's where you screwed up," Georgia said as if she was psychic. "You let it get emotional."

I stood, tired of watching the security feed. "It should also be emotional, G. That's why you're screwed up."

Leaving her to chew on that, I made my way to the bar and ordered a Scotch from the club's newest bartender.

"You giving a demonstration tonight?" Ariel asked.

I smiled tightly and shook my head. "I'm sitting out tonight."

"That's too bad." She leaned over the bar top conspiratorially. "I've heard about you. I was hoping to see you in action."

"I can't imagine what you've heard, because this isn't really my scene anymore." I swallowed the rest of my drink and ordered another.

"People say you're cold. Ruthless. That you push your subject to the edge, but that no one ever safes out."

I didn't like to remember that part of myself. Taking a

swig of my refill, I realized that if I was going to accomplish the task I'd been given, it might be my only choice. I had a decision to make. I needed this to be a clean break. I needed her to never want to look at me again. It was the only way to ensure Hammond would lose interest in her. Setting down my tumbler, I unbuttoned my shirt.

"Are there any subs here tonight?" I asked Ariel.

"That would be me," Georgia called from the doorway. "The rest are collared and their Masters aren't sharing."

I slid my shirt off, annoyed that she was my only option. But if I had to choose between taking a trip down fucking memory lane with her and Belle's safety, I knew where I stood.

"Any preferences?" I asked her.

"The prayer stool."

Of course, it was always at the top of her list. That was Georgia. She sought absolution through pain and found salvation in sin. "I'm using the cane."

"Dom's choice." But I could tell she was satisfied.

We crossed in silence to the corner of the room where the stool waited. Georgia knelt down, folding her hands in front of her.

"Is the pageantry necessary?" I asked as I lifted her skirt to reveal her bare ass.

"It is for me. I know exactly what you're doing," she whispered, "but if I'm going to put on a show, it's going to be a good one. By the way, your pet is here."

I paused for a moment, resisting the urge to turn and look for Belle. Instead of giving in, I reached forward and took the cane from a hook on the wall. It felt strange to have the reedy instrument in my palm. I hadn't used one in years and then it had been playful. Georgia didn't want a game and Belle needed to be scared.

It sliced through the air and cracked across Georgia's ass cheeks, immediately leaving an angry red streak on her pale skin. She barely reacted, maintaining her blasphemous position. She lasted three more stripes before her knees buckled and she had to grip the leather armrest.

"Enough?" I asked in a harsh voice. A kind Dom would soothe her injuries with a gentle touch, but I wasn't a good Dom and Georgia was far more depraved than a typical sub.

She shook her head.

I struck her three more times before I saw tears leak from the corner of her eyes. Dropping the cane, I tugged her skirt back into place and helped her stand. Before I could leave her, Georgia threw her arms around me and kissed my cheek, whispering in my ear. "Thank you for not holding back."

I peeled her back, revulsion and concern warring inside me. In some ways, she was my only friend. The only person who truly knew who I was and what I was capable of. It made me feel responsible for her well-being. But Georgia didn't want to be helped. Whatever balance her life needed, I would never give it to her.

Turning away from the corner and wishing I could leave this part of my past there, I found myself staring into Belle's tear-filled eyes.

I'd expected her to come. I'd known she would and that

she would witness this. But knowing hadn't prepared me for the look on her face like she didn't know who I was.

She was the one person I wanted to know me, and I had to end things like this.

I walked toward her, picking up my shirt on the way. This needed to be done publicly. It was the only way to be certain Hammond would hear of it. But doing that meant forcing her to endure the humiliation of my actions.

"You came," I said as I slipped my shirt back on and began to button it.

"I thought you were crazy," she whispered, "asking me to come here. But now I see that isn't the case at all. You're only cruel."

She pivoted away from me, and I caught her arm.

*Get it together, Price.* Stopping her wasn't part of the plan.

"I needed to blow off some steam," I lied. "I didn't think you'd be up for it."

"Is that what you want?" she asked in horror. "What happened to it being about pleasure?"

"It can't always be about that." I shrugged, unable to meet her eyes.

To my surprise, she kicked off her heels and reached for the zipper on her dress. "Is this what you need, Smith? You want me to get naked, so you can beat me and prove what a big man you are?"

I smacked her hand away. That was not how I wanted this to play out. Regardless of what she thought, she belonged to me and I wasn't going to share her with anyone. I certainly wasn't going to push tonight any further. There was no need. I sensed her pain, feeling it as acutely as if I had been the one under the cane. The scene had done the trick.

But Belle wasn't the type of woman to run away crying. She would punish me first.

"C'mon," she mocked. "Take out your stick and let's go."

"I don't want this with you."

That stopped her in her tracks. Her hand fell limply to her side, her lip beginning to quiver. "What do you want with me?"

"Nothing." It hurt worse because it was the truth and a lie. I wanted her to leave. I wanted her to run. Just as much as I wanted to give all of myself to her.

A single tear escaped down her cheek, and she wiped it angrily away. "That can be arranged."

But she didn't make a move to leave.

I wanted to ask her if she was okay. I wanted to walk her to her car. I wanted to take her home and make love to her until she forgot what she had seen. Instead I forced a glowering look on my face. "Well? What are you waiting for?"

"Nothing. Absolutely nothing."

Snatching her shoes from the floor, she dashed back toward the velvet-lined corridor that led outside. My eyes followed her progress, my body fighting me to go after her. Rather, I walked slowly back to the private office, feeling Ariel's shocked eyes on me.

I didn't watch as she left the club, even though Georgia had turned Velvet's security cameras on her. Letting her go had been difficult, but seeing her actually do it might prove impossible.

"It was the right choice." Georgia's sharp voice interrupted my thoughts.

"But is it one I can live with?" I said softly. My animosity toward her had fled the club along with Belle. "Don't answer that."

"Hammond suspects you two are involved. Your penchant for disappearing hasn't gone unnoticed. Neither will tonight's events. It's the best move you can make."

I rounded on her, my hands clenching into fists. "This isn't a game."

"It is a game," she shot back, "to Hammond at least. You can't get away with not playing. Not if you want to take her off the board."

She was right, and I hated it. I'd hoped we could ride out the storm longer, so Belle knew exactly where she stood. But warning her of what to expect would only have undermined the effectiveness of my strategy.

"What are you going to do now?"

"I need to call our partners." I forced myself to focus on the next rational move.

"There's no need to involve them." Georgia perched on her desk and crossed her arms over her voluptuous chest.

"Who the hell do you think forced this course of action?" I had my mobile out before she could respond.

Georgia huffed and slid off the desk. "Don't put too much stock in their ability to protect her."

"What choice do I have?" I asked gruffly as she walked out of the room.

"Smith." The voice on the other end sounded surprised to hear from me.

"Let's cut the bullshit," I said, skipping through the obligatory pleasantries. He didn't need me kissing his ass.

"I didn't expect to hear from you directly."

I bet he didn't. "Look, it's done. I cut her loose."

"You've made a wise choice."

"I don't give a damn what you think of my choice. She's still of interest to Hammond. There's no one I can trust to keep tabs on her."

"And you want me to?" he guessed.

"No one would second-guess your motivations," I reminded him.

"It's done. Is there anything else?"

"Yes, consider speaking with me before you pull something like this again." I was losing my cool now. What did it matter if another ally wanted me dead when I was already on someone else's hit list?

"You work for me." The friendly tone evaporated from his voice.

"I don't work for anyone." I hung up before he could respond. I'd gotten what I needed from him, and even if I found his tactics questionable, I trusted his word. That wasn't something that was easy for me, but I didn't have a choice. Not where Belle was concerned. He'd watch out for her and his resources were unparalleled. He was the best chance I stood at keeping her from Hammond's grasp.

"You know how to make friends," Georgia remarked, lowering herself carefully into a chair.

"Do you want some water or something?" I asked out of

obligation. I didn't have to imagine the condition she was already in.

"Let's not pretend that was anything more than a calculated move," she said with a snort. "You did what you had to do."

I had, and I was the one who had to live with it.

# CHAPTER SIX

*L*ife became an endless cycle. Go to work, obsess over launch, go home, obsess over launch, sleep. Rinse. Lather. Repeat. After a week I'd managed to get myself into a comfortable, mind-numbing rhythm that allotted almost no time to think about Smith. Almost.

Anger was swiftly shifting to sadness. Because despite the jam-packed schedule I'd been keeping, I was still aware of the fact that he hadn't called. Not to explain himself. Not to apologize. The lack of communication only confirmed my biggest fear: I meant nothing to him. I had only been another toy in his collection. Ignoring the piles of to-do lists cluttering my desk, I shot off an email to my brother, the only other lawyer I knew, to discuss my options. My fledgling business was tangled up with a man that I never wanted to see again.

Lola sashayed into the office a minute later with an oversized white leather tote hooked in the crook of her elbow and her arms brimming over with a stack of fashion magazines. She dropped it all onto one of the empty shelves littering the room. Stepping back, she surveyed the space, sizing it up after being absent for most of the week attending her last semester of classes. As usual she looked like she'd stepped from one of the pages of those fashion magazines, outfitted in a chic, loose tan sweater with a Burberry scarf knotted loosely at her neck. She'd paired skinny jeans with leather riding boots to complete the classic look that gave her the air of a woman much more sophisticated and worldly than your average twenty-two-year-old.

My mobile rang and I snatched it up. When I saw it wasn't Smith, I told myself that my lightning fast answering reflex had nothing to do with hope. I held no hope that there were any emotional ties binding me to him, which was why I should have been glad to see my brother's name on the screen.

Lola raised her eyebrows, no doubt responding to my frantic movements, and I smiled, holding up a finger to give me a moment to take the call.

"I just read your email," John said as soon as I answered. I pictured him in his leather desk chair facing his office window, which afforded a stunning view from one of the top floors of the Gherkin. "Can you pop by the office this afternoon for a few minutes?"

"Yes," I responded automatically. I wanted this dealt with as soon as possible. "How's two?"

"Perfect. I'll let security know to send you straight up."

We hung up without saying goodbye. As far as I could tell, pleasantries and affectionate farewells were reserved for siblings who had actually grown up in the same household.

Setting a reminder on my phone, I turned my attention back to sorting through the various contacts I needed to reach out to. Bless still had no inventory and procuring clothing was going to be as vital as securing clients. When I began scribbling a list down from the computer screen, Lola cleared her throat softly.

"So do you want to tell me what's wrong?" she asked, dropping onto a stool by my makeshift desk.

I glanced up, fingers freezing over the keyboard, and blinked. Did I? I'd managed to avoid Edward's check-in calls for the better part of the weekend, and Clara was lost in baby land, which meant I hadn't actually talked about the break-up with anyone. But confessing the situation would mean sharing the backstory and that was complicated.

"I'm behind," I answered instead. That was true, at least. I was just busy. So busy I hadn't even said hello to her.

*You're a machine,* and not in a good way. It's like working with robot Belle around here." Lola folded her arms over her chest, shaking her sleek dark hair. "Something is up."

"Yeah, we're supposed to be launching this company in two months," I snapped, "and I don't have inventory or a website or a marketing plan."

"But you have a partner," Lola reminded me. "Stop trying to do it all yourself and let me tackle the website and marketing."

I relaxed back in my seat and nodded. She had a point. "I had a boyfriend. Now I don't."

It was all she really needed to know. All any woman ever needed to know, and judging by the way her pink lips pressed into a grim line, she didn't need to hear more. "I get it, but don't switch into survival mode. So the cad is out of the picture, you still have a lot of people who have your back, and I'm one of them. You aren't doing this all by yourself."

"Wow, for a minute, I could have sworn Clara was here," I teased.

Lola straightened up and smirked, tossing her hair back over a slender shoulder. "*We are sisters,* even if she has much better taste in men."

"It sounds as if I'm not the only one with man trouble," I noted. It wasn't surprising exactly. There were too many Philips in the world and not enough Alexanders.

"Not trouble exactly. I'm just not interested. I'm either supposed to be impressed by the size of their portfolio or the size of their ego. Apparently they didn't get the memo that size only matters when it comes to one thing."

"And then there's the fact that Clara married the King of England," I added.

"It does put life into rather harsh perspective," Lola agreed with a laugh. "Mother doesn't understand why I haven't snagged my own world leader. Of course, she doesn't know that the last time I was forward with a man, he came out of the closet five minutes later. Obviously I need to focus on my career."

"You did Edward a favor," I told her, smiling at the

memory. "But I'm with you. Who needs a man to take over the world?"

"That, I'll drink to." She picked up an empty Starbucks cup and tossed it into the rubbish bin.

"Sadly, we haven't stocked the office bar yet," I said dryly.

"An oversight which will be remedied shortly. For now, I'm taking you to lunch." She held up a hand when I opened my mouth to protest. "A *business* lunch. Divide and conquer. That's how we're going to do this."

I grabbed my bag and followed her out the door, locking it behind us. She was right. I couldn't do this alone, and if I was going to pay Smith's investment back and finally be free, a battle strategy was definitely in order.

A FEW HOURS LATER, I made my way across town, my mind spinning with all of Lola's ideas. I was so preoccupied that I nearly walked past the security checkpoint at the entrance of my brother's building.

"Miss?" A uniformed guard stopped me and gestured toward my purse.

"Oops." I unzipped it and held it out for his inspection.

He peeked in with a flashlight. "Are you carrying a mobile phone? We need to check that."

"Um, probably." I rifled around and came up empty. "I must have left it at the office."

"Do you have an appointment?" he asked dubiously.

He thinks you're a flake. What professional showed up

for a meeting without a mobile? I seriously needed to get my act together if I was going to evolve into a business mogul. I dug out my wallet and showed him my ID. "I do. Annabelle Stuart. I'm meeting with John Stuart."

"Head on up," he said after checking his list, adding, "you do know your way?"

"I'll be fine," I reassured him, taking off for the lift. Due to the mortifying security check, it was nearly two and I didn't have a mobile to let my brother know that I'd be late. It was exactly two when I reached his floor and tore up to the reception desk.

"I'm here for John Stuart," I told the girl behind the desk in a breathless voice.

"Mr. Stuart is expecting you." She gestured to the left. John's law firm was the exact opposite of Smith's small private practice. Nearly a dozen lawyers practiced here, filling the roles of solicitors and barristers alike.

"Belle." He rose politely as I entered, bowing slightly and tugging at the cuffs of his Harris Tweed jacket. Everything from his thinning hair to his clothing choices and odd adherence to decorum made him appear much older than thirty-two.

I never knew what to do around him. Shake his hand. Curtsy. In all fairness, he'd never been anything but unfailingly kind to me, despite the awkward favoritism our father had shown me. No doubt owing to my mother's interference.

"How are you?" he asked, once again proving himself the essence of civilized formality.

"Busy," I admitted, not sure if I could handle a round of small talk. "You?"

"I've also been quite busy."

We sat for a moment in awkward silence before he glanced at his computer screen. "I was quite surprised to hear you were starting a business. It doesn't seem like something your mother would approve of."

"She doesn't," I said flatly. I didn't miss the way his eyes tightened as he spoke of her. My mother had always made her disapproval of my choices known in private. She'd been publicly vocal about her disapproval of John's existence. Wicked stepmother indeed.

"I can empathize with the position you find yourself in then." His tone had softened. We both understood how it felt to be unwanted. Although, in comparison, he'd had it much worse. After his mother had died, my father had remarried. His new wife, my *loving* mother, had immediately shipped John off to boarding school, and he had stayed there until university. "It should make Christmas quite interesting."

"I propose we let Ann enjoy her estate by herself this Christmas," I suggested. It was the first year I'd be single, and while Philip had never been much emotional support, he'd been a distraction at least. I had no interest in spending the day being analyzed and found wanting.

"It is *your* estate," John reminded me in a clipped tone. "Perhaps *you* could un-invite *her*."

"Do you recall the end of Jane Eyre? I wouldn't put it past her to try to roast us both alive." The joke lightened the mood a bit but didn't fully erase the implication of his words. John had inherited my father's title as his only son, a right granted to him by British law, but I'd wound up inheriting the family estate. I had no doubt my mother had forced our father to disregard John in all other ways as well.

"So is your mother this unwanted investor?" John asked.

"Thankfully no." I shook my head, actually laughing at the thought. If my mother had any money, she wouldn't give it to me. "But unfortunately I have, or rather had, a personal relationship with the current investor."

"And now you don't," John guessed, but he didn't press for details. It was probably obvious from the red flushing across my cheeks what kind of relationship it had been. "This isn't normally my area of expertise. I don't work directly with clients any more since I became one of the firm's barristers."

"Oh," I said in a small voice. My legal problems were about to get a lot more expensive if John was unable to handle the issue.

"I am able to handle litigation," he clarified. "I generally don't though, so you might want to seek a second opinion because you might not like mine."

"Fair enough." I braced myself for his response, breath caught in my throat.

"As an investor, he has little claim on your actual business. He may choose to divest and force repayment, but from what you told me in your email, his interest is entirely financial. He shouldn't interfere. If you feel that you want him out, I'd repay the investment and be certain he's not written into any legal documents as a shareholder moving forward."

It wasn't the worst news he could have given, but it wasn't exactly what I wanted to hear. I suppose I'd hoped John could offer some sort of miraculous solution that hadn't occurred to me. But Smith was part of my life until I could buy him out.

"You're disappointed," John noted.

I dismissed his concern with a wave of my hand. "It's a feeling I'm used to."

Our eyes met, and for the first time in many years, I saw the same painful memories I'd carried reflected in someone else's eyes. We'd never spoken of our father's death. It was the ghost that no one spoke of in my family.

"A word of advice?" John offered. "Not as your lawyer, but as a...brother. Move on. Don't feel guilty for taking what has been given to you and don't apologize."

"No apologies," I repeated.

John's gaze faded into the distance as he reiterated, "None."

# CHAPTER SEVEN

*A*ndrew's office was everything mine was not. Perched on one of the highest floors of his building, it loomed over the city's financial district. To be honest, the whole thing reeked of a sort of masculine inferiority syndrome. Why else erect something that looked like a towering dick in the middle of London than if you couldn't get yours up?

"I've reviewed the documents and I see no issue with proceeding," he informed me as he reappeared. One of my oldest friends from law school, the years—and corporate law—hadn't been kind to him. It showed in the lines creasing his forehead.

Perhaps I would be similarly worn down if I'd pursued a more traditional practice. Although it hardly seemed fair that life had been so hard on him when I was the one entangled with criminals.

"Then everything is in order?" I asked, ready to be done with this business.

"Legally," Andrew agreed. He gestured for me to take a seat before crossing the room to pour two Scotches. "Personally, I would be a bit more concerned."

I took the drink he offered me without responding. I knew exactly what the personal stakes were, and I'd already made sacrifices to ensure whatever chaos ensued from finalizing the sale of my holdings in Velvet would be restricted to me. But Andrew was a decent man. He'd advised me on difficult cases before, which is why I'd entrusted him to handle this one swiftly and privately.

"Hammond isn't likely to roll over on this, Smith." He took a long sip and shook his head. The implication was clear. He couldn't understand what I was thinking. Of course, he'd also never been as mixed up with a client as I was with my boss.

I swirled the amber liquid in the bottom of the glass as I considered how to respond. I trusted Andrew as far as I trusted any professional acquaintance. "I don't expect him to. But there is a personal reason that I want out of the club. A couple, actually."

It didn't take a genius to guess that I wanted free from the sordid enterprises Hammond had built throughout London. It probably also didn't take much to piece together that my father had been a victim of Hammond's organized crime empire and that the odds were I would suffer a similar fate. Most of my associates had figured that out long before I did. What might be harder to comprehend was why I was purposefully drawing attention to myself now.

"I'm still retained by Hammond," I finished.

"But are you in his good graces?" Andrew asked. He placed his empty glass on the side table and leaned forward. "You have to know this is suicide."

I did know that. The clock had been ticking since last spring when I'd found myself in the precarious position of choosing sides. "I wish I could explain myself. Doing this with the club will hardly matter, but it's important for me to sever ties with Velvet."

"She must be something." He rubbed his chin with a sigh.

So he had guessed. While most might assume I wanted out of the twisted birthright my father had left me, Andrew saw through me. "Tell me. Is it obvious because you know me or because I've lost my touch?"

"Lucky guess," he assured me. "You are as unreadable as ever, my friend."

I wanted to breath a sigh of relief, but instead I tipped my head, smiling tightly.

"This will bring attention to her as well." His forehead creased as his tone grew serious.

"I've taken measures." He didn't need to know more than that. While he might be trustworthy, I'd learned a few things from my unlikely partnership with Georgia. People could be bought. People could be sold out. And people, especially men, had a tendency to spill secrets when they got a chance to put their dicks in a warm, welcoming pussy.

"You're smart, even if this a particularly stupid move. I certainly hope there won't be fall-out."

There would be. The only choice I had was to be

outside of the blast radius—a feat which I already knew was impossible. But keeping Belle far from the danger was something I could control. No matter the cost.

"You've considered that if he makes a move, it might not be a physical attack. Your entire career is in his hands. There's more ways to kill a man than to put a bullet through his head."

"I'm prepared for that as well." There were no more reassurances I could offer him. Even if I had been willing to lay out my entire plan on the spot, it would risk too many others in the process. "I wish I could be upfront with you. Your concern is touching."

"You're a good man. I simply want the best for you." He held out his hand, and I shook it firmly.

That wasn't a sentiment I was accustomed to hearing. If Andrew knew me better—if he knew the things I'd done—the thought would never have occurred to him. But there was a small comfort to be taken from his words. I could never hope to absolve myself of the sins of my past but trying had to count for something.

Andrew patted my shoulder as I left his office. I'd thought that some of my burden would be lifted when I relinquished my claim to Velvet, but instead it felt heavier than ever before. The move had come at a price, and while I'd been willing to pay it, I still felt its sting.

Stepping inside the lift, I toyed with the mobile in my pocket. There was only one person I wanted to call to share this news with, and she was absolutely off-limits. That was the missing piece. The reason that finally snipping a thread that linked me to Hammond hadn't been the victory I'd expected. No doubt Belle would have shot off a smart-ass remark that redirected my attention from the inevitable consequences of my actions to thoughts of spending the evening taming her attitude. My cock stiffened a little at the fantasy. No amount of rationale could convince him that I'd made the right move.

The lift came to a stop on the next floor, and this time when the doors opened, I blinked, wondering if my imagination had finally gotten the better of me. It was going to be a long ride down the remaining flights if my daydreams were becoming so vivid.

But judging from the way she froze on the spot, confusion turning into pain, she wasn't an illusion. Belle paused, as if considering her next move, before she walked in and took up the farthest possible spot in the compartment. Her gaze remained trained on the buttons as we began to descend once more.

*Of all the lifts in London, she walks into mine.*

Her perfume lingered in the air, and it took a considerable amount of effort to restrain myself. My dick was having none of it, having grown rock hard at the sight of her. The burden I'd felt entering the lift seemed to lift and deposit itself directly onto my chest. How did you tell a woman that you hurt her to protect her?

I wanted to shove her against the wall, hitch up her skirt, and claim what was mine. Because Belle Stuart was mine. I'd let her walk away, but I hadn't let her go. She wouldn't stop me. That much I was sure of her. She might be managing to pretend I didn't exist, but I could see it in her body language. In the way she rubbed her calf nervously against her shin. In the slight tap of her fingers on the metal rail that ran along the perimeter of the space. In the sharp intake of breath that came every few seconds.

She was as aware of my presence as I was of hers. Her body responding to the memories I'd given it. If I lifted her skirt and shoved my hand between her legs, she'd be as wet as I was hard.

Just one taste. One stolen kiss. One bite to her pale shoulder. One hand wrapped around her slender throat. One more moment.

But giving in would undo everything I'd worked for, and it would make the pain I'd caused her worthless. She had more value than that. I owed her more respect than to toy with her.

When we reached the lobby, I exited without a word. It was easier that way.

For her at least.

# CHAPTER EIGHT

*L*ola descended on me as soon as I made it back to the office, her obvious excitement distracting me from my run-in with Smith. I was barely through the door before she had me cornered. She twisted her hands, bouncing on her heels. The girl was practically vibrating. Sidling past her, I dropped my bag on the floor and sank into my chair.

"Well?" I prompted, concerned that she might explode if I didn't give her some attention. The last thing I needed was to have to repaint. Closing my eyes, I tried to focus on her and not my heartbreaking encounter in the lift.

"I didn't want to say anything before because I figured it was a long shot. But then I got a call, and oh my god, Belle! This is it!" she gushed.

I opened one eye and stared at her, wondering if I'd missed something vital in what she'd just told me. "Forgive me, but what is it?"

"*Trend!*" she exclaimed, glaring at me like I should know this.

Despite the nonsensical stream of information spewing from her, this got my attention. I sat up, both eyes open, and waited.

"Abigail Summers's assistant just phoned me. They love the idea behind Bless and want to do an exclusive editorial."

"*Trend?*" I repeated. Now I understood why Lola was barely coherent.*Trend* was the most widely recognized fashion magazine in the world and had been for nearly fifty years. As a start-up, we wouldn't have been able to afford an ad on their website. A magazine editorial was beyond my wildest fantasies. "Oh my god!"

Tears spilled down my cheeks even as I began to laugh. It was full-blown hysteria. Here we were sitting in an empty office space. No website. No inventory. No customers. And somehow we'd managed to land an opportunity half of the fashion world would kill for.

"How did this happen?" I finally managed.

"A professor I'm working with this year used to be editorial staff," Lola explained. "She gave me the contact info and told me Abigail was looking to spotlight up-and-coming female entrepreneurs. It's part of a whole girl power theme they're focused on this year."

"I can't believe this." And I couldn't. It was as if the universe had taken pity on me and dropped a gift in my lap.

"The only catch is that you need to be in New York by Tuesday," Lola said.

My smile evaporated. "Wait, what?"

"The story is as much about you as it is about Bless." Lola shrugged her shoulders as if this made perfect sense.

Except that it didn't. In the fashion world, I was a nobody. My greatest contribution to that world so far was a couple of maxed-out credit cards spent during irresponsible shopping sprees. "What about you? You should take the interview."

Lola's background at university, not to mention her legacy as the daughter of two self-made millionaires, made her the perfect candidate for a major magazine piece.

"I have school," she reminded me. "Plus, Bless is your company."

"It's our company," I corrected her.

"You're generous," she said. "It will be someday when I've fulfilled my end of the deal. That much I can promise you. But this is still your baby. You had the vision. Besides you have a great story. Abigail loved it. Jilted by her fiancé, a bride-to-be ditches the no-good jerk and starts the next big thing in modern fashion merchandizing."

"When you put it like that, it does sound exciting. Except look around, Bless is pretty much still an idea." Nothing confirmed the validity of this more than the barren space surrounding us.

"In today's market, ideas are currency—and currency is still money," Lola informed me.

"You're taking very different classes than I did in school," I said with a smirk.

"Look, you are going to New York, and you're going to prove what a badass you truly are. No second-guessing yourself now. You're going to blow Abigail Summers away." Lola tilted her head, daring me to challenge her.

"It's not like I'll actually meet with Abigail," I said. I needed to align my enthusiasm with Lola's. This was an amazing chance. But keeping a level head also seemed a necessity.

"No, you will," she corrected me, flying into another frenzied announcement. "The whole thing is like a conversation between the two of you. The magazine spotlights the business while the interview is more of a mentoring session."

I lost the ability to speak. There was no way I was prepared for this. I'd spent the last week gathering the basic info. I'd rented an office. I had an elevator pitch. None of that was enough to impress someone with Abigail's reputation.

Lola's eyes narrowed. "Why do you look like I just gave you a death sentence?"

"I'm not certain you didn't."

"*Trend* is taking care of most of the travel arrangements. I'll handle the rest." She snapped into decision-making mode. "I'll also draw up a bunch of talking points you can use to discuss the brand and our plans. But don't forget, she wants to mentor. Massage her ego a little and get her feedback."

She had a point. If all else failed, flattery would get me through.

"While you're gone, I'll finalize the website plans with the web designer and start reaching out to the designers," she continued. "Now this is important. Do you have stuff to wear? It has to be this season!"

I could tell by the way she looked me over as she said this that my choice of outfit today had worried her. I wore a classic ivory blouse and navy pencil skirt. There was nothing sexy or exciting about it, but I had owned it for three years and it still worked. It wasn't the height of current fashion, however.

"I have clothes." I swallowed hard on my own words. I had clothes given to me by Smith. My wardrobe not only had some current pieces, it had all of them. Without a doubt, they would impress Abigail Summers. I just had to bring myself to wear them. I'd shoved them in the back of my closet and studiously avoided them since that night at Velvet. Now I would be forced to take a huge leap forward in my career with the burden of my obligation to Smith weighing me down. John's words from earlier in the afternoon echoed in my mind.

*No guilt.* I was going to have that tattooed on my forearm.

"You gain a day heading to the U.S., but you're going to be exhausted, so you leave on Monday."

"Fuck, fuck, fuck," I said under my breath, mentally running through the list of things I needed to have done before I took off. Manicure, at the very least. Maybe a wax. My hair had gotten longer due to being distracted by Smith and then the business. There was no way to get into the hairdresser on time.

"Relax," Lola instructed me. "You have the whole weekend to get everything done. And try to take a minute and be happy. Don't get too caught up in your to-do list that you miss out on the amazing."

I lunged for her, wrapping her in a tight hug. "Thank you!"

"Thank you for trusting me to be part of this." She squeezed back. "I've got things here. Oh, and I'm going to call the landlord and have him change the lock. I watched you lock the door earlier and it popped right open when I got back from our lunch. I think it's broken."

"Was anything missing?" I asked with a frown.

"No. I checked," she reassured me. "Your phone was sitting right out on the desk. Thank god this is a quiet neighborhood."

"Speaking of, I need to get to my neighborhood and to my closet."

Lola pecked me on the cheek, and I rushed toward the door.

"Hey," she called after me, "you deserve this."

Hell yes, I did. Nobody was going to hold me back anymore. Not even myself.

THE SENSUAL, upbeat rhythm of Samba music filled my flat by the time I arrived there with freshly manicured hands. I couldn't resist swaying my hips as I made my way into the small living room I shared with my aunt. Jane grinned wildly as I joined her, holding out her hands. I took them nervously, allowing her to lead me into a few steps until I tripped onto the rug. Jane snorted as I stumbled and fell onto the sofa. She continued moving with the beat, her silk house robe swirling wildly around her. When the song ended, she plopped down beside me.

"I'm also afraid to tell you that it's Friday evening." Jane pursed her lips knowingly. "I wouldn't want you to go back to the office."

Jane hadn't pressed me when I came home a week ago crying. She hadn't needed an explanation at all. And she'd managed to keep her mouth shut about the insane number of hours I'd been spending on Bless. Apparently that grace period was over, but I didn't care. I'd spent the last two hours allowing myself to celebrate the biggest achievement in my very short career's history.

I pulled the latest copy of Trend from my tote bag and threw it in her lap.

"Ever read this?" I asked. Now that I was the one brimming over with the news, I wondered how Lola had been able to remain so composed.

"Not for years." Jane paged through it, stopping occasionally to scan an article. "I haven't exactly followed fashion trends for the past twenty years. It's very liberating."

I rolled my eyes at her insinuation. Jane supported my idea even if she didn't quite understand its appeal. "It's my job to follow them," I reminded her. "Anyway, they want to feature Bless."

"That's wonderful!" Jane cried, dragging me into a hug. When I pulled back, tears sparkled in her eyes.

"Don't do that," I warned her, already feeling wet heat prickling in my own. "Or I'll cry."

"You've worked so hard and you've picked yourself back up. I couldn't be prouder."

A lump formed in my throat, and no matter how hard I swallowed, it didn't budge. I'd spent most of my life searching for my mother's approval. Jane had filled that void for me. Making her proud meant more than anything.

"I leave for New York on Monday."

"This just keeps getting better." Jane's eyes twinkled, but this time it wasn't the glisten of tears. It was mischief. "The city that never sleeps. What fun."

"Business," I corrected her. "It will probably be a few meetings and some room service."

"That won't do." Jane shook her platinum head. "And you'll never get away with it anyway. It's impossible to go to New York without it getting under your skin. It's so alive there, it's infectious."

"I'll use protection," I said flatly. There had been a time when visiting the city had been on my bucket list. Knowing I was going there alone, and for a business trip, sucked some of the flavor out of the opportunity. And more importantly, the trip was about Bless. Now wasn't the time to be distracted by romanticizing the city. Not when I needed to be laser-focused on the task at hand.

"Before you leave the country," Jane said, her tone taking on a seriousness that meant I was about to get an earful about something, "call Edward. That boy is beside himself. He's so worried about you that he stopped by here last night."

"I will," I promised sheepishly.

Jane's penetrating gaze saw right through me. "He's not going to rub it in. He cares about you."

"I just wanted to pretend nothing was wrong," I admitted in a low voice.

"No, you wanted to avoid what was wrong." Jane knitted her soft, papery fingers through mine.

I nodded, knowing she'd nailed it. "I should call him."

"Sooner rather than later," she suggested.

"Sooner," I echoed. It was time to stop avoiding what I'd been through and focus my energy on what I had in front of me. My friends. My business. And a trip to New York City.

# CHAPTER NINE

*M*onday morning found me with bags packed, waiting for a car service outside my flat. With any luck, Heathrow would be calm enough that I would have time to grab a cup of tea before my flight, but I wasn't counting on it. The driver was already five minutes late, and with each second that passed, I thought of something new to worry about. Did I have my passport? A check of my bag confirmed I did. Had I packed a toothbrush? They probably had those in New York if I'd forgotten. Was I going crazy? Yes. Definitely yes. When the car finally pulled to the curb, I snatched up my luggage as the window rolled down, revealing a familiar face.

"Your drivers have arrived," Edward called jovially.

"My drivers are late," I scolded him, not feeling even remotely upset. He'd been over the moon when I'd finally called him. He hadn't even mentioned Smith. Undoubtedly Lola had kept the rest of our tight-knit group abreast that there was trouble in paradise.

"Do you know how hard it is to get His Royal Highness out of bed?" Lola yelled from the driver's seat as I slung my bag inside the back and slid in. I'd opted for a comfortable knit dress that still looked professional. I had no idea who would be meeting me at JFK International, but I wasn't taking any chances. I'd even worn stockings.

"In my defense, I had no idea there were two six o'clocks," Edward said, shifting so his arm was casually resting on the armrest between the seats.

"Try looking at a clock," Lola suggested as she merged onto the motorway.

The good-natured bickering continued between the two of them, nearly lulling me back to sleep.

"You have your flight information, right?" Lola asked.

I shook the cobwebs out of my head. "I have what you sent me."

"A driver will meet you at the baggage claim and get you to your hotel. Abigail's assistant is supposed to send that info this afternoon, so check your email when you land." Lola rattled off a half-dozen other instructions and I smiled and nodded. It was all information I already knew, but I appreciated how earnest she was about this trip.

"I can't believe I can't get either of you to come with me." I'd tried. Lola had been clear it was impossible, but Edward's refusal had been more puzzling. "Too busy with matters of state? Couldn't ensure you'd have a security team available?"

Edward peeked back at me, shaking his head, and gave me the side eye. "There was no time to arrange a proper welcoming parade. A prince must have his standards."

"You are so full of yourself." Lola smacked his shoulder, her eyes never leaving the road.

"Of course, I am. I'm royalty," he shot back.

"Tell her the real reason," Lola demanded haughtily.

"I knew something was up." I pointed a finger at him. "You. Tell. Now."

"If you must know…" he trailed away.

"I must," I pressed. It wasn't like Edward to be so secretive. It was actually a good thing that he didn't have the same responsibilities as his brother. I wasn't entirely certain he could be trusted with classified information.

"David and I are meeting with Alexander," he admitted in a quiet voice.

"Finally!" I threw my hands up in the air. "I don't know why you've held out so long."

"He's not going to say no," Lola added, echoing the opinion I'd expressed to Edward at least a dozen times since he'd proposed to his boyfriend.

"It is slightly more complicated than cold feet," Edward said flatly.

My eyes narrowed. Edward had come out publicly almost a year ago and proposed to his longtime boyfriend a few months later. Despite pressure from Clara, David, and myself, he'd been dragging his feet on setting a date for months. "They might not be cold, but they're certainly slow."

"So explain it to us," Lola said.

"I can't." This time his refusal was straightforward and firm. Judging from the way Lola's head jolted in surprise, we were both taken back.

"What do you mean?" I said with a laugh. We'd never shared the more sordid details of our love lives. I really didn't think he wanted to hear about Smith's penchant for dominance. But neither of us had ever shied away from analyzing even the most mundane aspects of our relationship statuses.

"I mean, I can't." Edward ran a hand through his curly hair and slouched back into his seat, turning his gaze to stare out the window. "Please don't ask more."

Maybe I was wrong about his ability to keep secrets. Although I couldn't fathom what he was hiding from us now.

"Fine. Can I ask who your maid of honor is going to be?" I said, shifting the topic to clear the heavy tension in the cabin. "I have an idea if you need suggestions."

"I was thinking we might elope," Edward said. "How are you with the beach?"

"I'm good with that." Reaching forward, I put a hand on his shoulder. I wouldn't force him to tell me more, but I still wanted him to know that I was here for him. He took it and held it for the rest of the ride. We chattered about cakes and honeymoon locations, each of us avoiding the questions that had been left unanswered.

But as we pulled up to the drop-off lane at Heathrow, I couldn't help but wonder when relationships had gotten so complicated. There was a time when Clara and I kept nothing from one another. These days we barely had time to talk, and she'd never been terribly forthcoming about her private relationship with Alexander. Now Edward was shutting me out. It didn't diminish my love for either of them, but it did hurt, especially given how closed-off Smith had been about his personal life outside our relationship.

Uh-uh. My conscience interrupted me before I could descend into the spiral of self-doubt any further.

Edward popped out of the car and gave me a swift kiss on the cheek. We both did our best to ignore the number of travelers who stopped to snap a pic. It was one of the liabilities of being best friends with him.

"Tomorrow morning, they'll be reporting that you've gone straight," I whispered to him. I could see the tabloid covers now. Given the whirlwind I'd been privy to in the last year and a half, I could probably write headlines for them.

"Once you go gay, you never stray," he teased, passing me my bag from the backseat. "David will get a good laugh out of them."

Lola rolled her window down and blew me a kiss. "See you in a few days."

"I'll call you," I promised her.

"You better. See if you can get Abigail to take a selfie with you for our social media feeds."

I agreed, even though there was no way in hell I was going to embarrass myself by asking for that. Abigail Summers didn't strike me as the selfie type.

Inside the airport doors, I groaned when I saw the security line and found myself cursing Edward for not coming along once more. There would be no way I'd have to wait in that line with him at my side. Hauling my bag over to the ticketing counter, I handed my passport over to check my bag.

"Miss Stuart," she chirped, "how many bags will you be checking today?"

"Just one." I'd managed to cram it full of six pairs of shoes and a dozen more dresses.

"Very good. Here's your boarding pass. Since you're flying in first class, you can use the fast track security lane to the left."

I glanced down at my ticket in surprise. Apparently, *Trend* didn't mess around. "Thank you!"

My trip was already off to a great start. After bypassing most of the line, I not only had time for a cup of tea but a croissant as well in the airline's private lounge. Scanning through *The Telegraph*, I spotted familiar faces on the society page. Apparently Pepper Lockwood wasn't going to heed my warning and kick Philip to the curb. I stuffed the last flaky bite of pastry in my mouth and drained my tea. Those two deserved each other. I was certain it would be a long and painful union for the both of them. Smith had cured me of any lasting bitterness over Philip's betrayal. Or maybe he'd just replaced my bitterness over that break-up with bitterness over our own relationship ending.

The few times I'd flown overseas to visit a friend in Los Angeles, I'd been forced to do so in economy, which wasn't terrible on an international flight. Until I was seated in first class international. I was pretty sure I could ask for a kidney transplant and receive one. I opted to stretch across my seat like it was a luxurious divan while flight attendants brought hot towels and champagne. Lunch and breakfast were served on respectable bone china. Given that I was about to spend the next five years or so building a business,

I wasn't getting used to the treatment. Every dime would have to go right back into Bless to make it the success I envisioned.

But I was going to bloody well enjoy it now.

I'd brought my laptop, but after an hour spent reviewing the talking points Lola had prepared—which I had memorized before take-off—I abandoned the computer in favor of a smutty novel I'd grabbed from the airport bookstore. But reading about sex with a broken heart turned out to be a bad idea.

"Do you want this?" I asked the flight attendant as she delivered a refill on my champagne. I'd better slow down or I'd pass out before I could even claim I was jet lagged.

She glanced at the cover and shook her head, leaning down to whisper, "I already read that series. What did you think?"

"Not my cup of tea." It was best to leave it there. The champagne I'd consumed threatened to take over and spill the emotional tale.

"It is a little kinky." She bit her lips, blushing as she said it.

Poor thing. I could guess that her experience with kinky ended in those pages. I kept the opinion to myself and shoved it in the magazine holder.

The way I saw it, after my failed literary attempt and the disastrous exchange with the flight attendant, I could give in to the champagne and cry. Or I could use it to my advantage and fall asleep.

Neither option felt very empowering, but at least if I slept, I wouldn't have to ask for tissues.

A few hours later, I was gently shaken awake by the kind woman. She handed me back my book to store for landing. Looking out the window, I caught sight of the Statue of Liberty, which looked disappointingly small from this height. It was my first trip to the east coast of America, and if there was one reason I was happy to be going alone, it was so I could be an awful tourist without judgment.

JFK proved slightly less civilized than Heathrow. I shot off a text to Lola as soon as I was through customs.

BELLE: I thought there was going to be a cavity search. Americans take their airports very seriously.

There was no response and no email with the information she'd promised me, but there was a man holding a sign with my name on it in baggage claim. Underneath was scrawled Bless.

Bless was real. Today was the proof. I was across the pond on a business trip. For a split second, I wished Smith could be here to see that. The thought squeezed my heart, and I quickly dismissed it.

"I'm Annabelle Stuart," I told the man with the sign.

"Welcome to New York," he said in an accent I'd only heard on television. "Are you here for business or pleasure?"

"Business," I responded as he led me to the baggage carousel. I no longer mixed the two.

# CHAPTER TEN

*a*s the car hurtled through the narrow lanes, the driver honking impatiently, I tried to take in the city for the first time. The streets of New York were as crowded as I'd imagined they would be. Everywhere there was chaotic blend of colors and people, all rushing toward the next item on their daily schedule. It made my head hurt. London was by no means a quiet metropolis, but this was something entirely different. Life in all its wild vitality pulsed from every direction.

We flew past a park full of activity. Even leisure time felt rushed here. Sinking against my seat, I closed my eyes and took a deep breath. So the city intimidated me. Big deal. I wasn't exactly a wallflower. I was accustomed to high-pressure situations. I'd been the maid of honor at the most infamous wedding in history after all. Tension fueled my passion, and I would work that to my advantage.

A few minutes later, the car slowed to a merciful stop, and I peeked back out the window to find the bustling entrance to one of the largest, and grandest, hotels I'd ever seen.

"Are you certain we're in the right place?" I asked the driver, allowing my confusion to show. *Trend* had been the one to arrange my accommodations, but I had a hard time believing they set up relatively green entrepreneurs in such lavish quarters.

"My sheet says to deliver you to the Plaza," he informed me. "This is it."

"Okay," I managed, but the words were barely out of my mouth before he was out of the car. He circled to the back as a bellman opened my door and offered me his hand.

The kindly gentleman seemed unfazed by the fact that my mouth was hanging open. "Welcome to the Plaza, Miss."

"Thank you." I took his hand and clamped my mouth shut. I deserved to be here. At least that was how I was going to have to sell this to myself.

That was harder when I walked through the doors. Marble floors morphed into marble columns, leading to a sweeping staircase. Clusters of richly upholstered chairs perched on plush rugs dotted the lobby, and a massive crystal chandelier scattered light across the wide space. A bellhop wheeled a cart with my baggage past me, and I followed him to the hotel desk.

"Checking in?" the woman behind it asked in a pert voice. She studied me for a moment before her eyes softened. I had the feeling I'd just passed a test.

"Annabelle Stuart." I handed her my passport and unzipped my wallet to retrieve my credit card.

"Oh yes, Miss Stuart." Her tone completely changed as she checked the computer screen. "We have you in the Hardenbergh Terrace Suite on the Penthouse level."

I bit the inside of my cheek, not wanting to sound like an idiot by asking another person if they were mistaken. Maybe I wasn't the only Annabelle Stuart arriving in New York today.

"It's on the twentieth floor. Your key card will grant you access. Please keep it with you at all times. The Plaza values the privacy of its guests, so security may ask to see it on occasion. Geoffrey, your personal butler, is available to you twenty-four hours a day should you require assistance."

I held out my credit card, suddenly more afraid to have her run it. It carried a limit that probably didn't cover the entrance fee to a place like this. To my relief, she waved it away.

"Everything has been taken care of. Geoffrey will show you to your suite." She beckoned across the lobby, and a man came forward dressed in a long tailcoat and white gloves. He looked as though he'd just stepped from the pages of an old novel.

"Miss Stuart." He tipped his head politely and lifted my bags from the trolley while I checked for an earpiece. Both the receptionist and the butler acted as if they'd been waiting all day for my arrival, and while I was positive I was about to make a splash in the business world, I hadn't done it yet.

As he led me toward the private lift off the lobby, I considered pinching myself. Maybe I was dreaming. Of course, I wouldn't put it past Lola to name drop to secure me above-average accommodations. But while I might be close personal friends with the British Monarchy, I was no princess. Something wasn't adding up.

It wasn't until the butler pressed the button for the twentieth floor that the pieces started to form a sickening picture. As the floor numbers lit up in swift succession, carrying me toward the top of the Plaza, my stomach dropped out. Suspicion turned into nauseating certainty as the lift doors slid open to my floor.

"I'm at your service during your stay," Geoffrey reminded me as he swept a key card over the lock. I mumbled something unintelligible in response. "Pardon?"

But Geoffrey wasn't getting clarification today. As I stepped into the suite, my eyes landed on the room's other occupant—the last person I wanted to see.

And the person I wanted to see more than anyone in the world.

Smith towered before me, a brutal pillar of masculinity, mercilessly clothed in a perfectly tailored suit. His strong jaw tensed slightly as our gazes met, his green irises flashing with possessiveness as he took me in. I knew the secrets he shielded behind those eyes as well as I knew the perfectly hewn body hidden under his clothes. His hands curled into fists as though he was trying to keep himself away from me. That desire was entirely mutual.

"Mr. Price," Geoffrey greeted him as he stepped in behind me. "Should I deliver these to the master bedroom or the guest room?"

Smith's face went blank as if Geoffrey had begun to speak in a foreign language. The message was obvious. A man like Smith Price didn't invite blondes to his suite to sleep in the guest room. The composed butler shifted uncomfortably on his heels.

"Leave them by the door," Smith instructed, holding out a wad of bills. "I'll see to Miss Stuart from here."

The words had an unwanted effect on me. My mouth went dry, my heart speeding up to a frenzy as I felt the magnetic tug of Smith's presence. It took every ounce of restraint I had to stay put and wait for the door to close behind me.

"I hope these accommodations are to your standards," Smith said stiffly.

So we were down to small talk. Of course we were. He'd gotten me into a hotel room in a strange city under false pretenses. I imagined he'd be bringing up the weather next. Anything to avoid the fact that he'd damn near kidnapped me. Or that he'd avoided me the last time we saw each other. Or that the last time we'd spoken it had been after watching him take a cane to Georgia Kincaid.

"My best friend lives in a palace. You're going to have to try harder to impress me," I snapped back.

"New city. Same attitude," he said dryly.

"Don't start with me," I warned him. "Answers now."

"I rearranged my travel to coincide with yours." He spoke as if this answered any of the questions I might have.

"Let's see. That doesn't tell me how you knew I would be in New York or how you hijacked me at the airport. Or most importantly, why you'd even bother?" I bit out. "We're over, remember? Or are you having a bout of amnesia?

You're not my controlling, overprotective boyfriend anymore. You decided you'd rather play with another toy."

It hurt to say that out loud. I'd been avoiding the reality of my situation since I'd left him at Velvet, saying only what I needed to silence the people in my life smart enough to guess things hadn't ended with Smith when he'd fired me from my job as his personal assistant.

"I never stopped being controlling or overprotective." He took a step closer. "Or your boyfriend."

"Then we're definitely interpreting the events of the last time we spoke to each other differently." I backed up, eager to maintain a safe distance from him. "Or is this just part of your game?"

"You're not a pawn to me, beautiful, but yes, this is part of a game."

"Then let me be clear: I'm not playing." If I moved quickly, I could grab my bags, but there was no way I'd make it into the lift before he reached me.

"I don't want you to."

"Then walk away again," I dared him. "Or better yet, let me leave now. You had no problem pushing me away before."

"There are people who want to hurt you, Belle, and as hard as it is for me to stay away from you, I will walk away before that happens."

"How can you say that?" I demanded. "What kind of life do you think I'll have without you in it?"

The thought was nearly too much to bear. I'd gotten through the last week through compartmentalizing. I'd tucked Smith and the memories we'd shared into boxes and tried to ignore their existence. But deep down, I knew the only reason I'd been able to do so was because I hadn't believed things were truly over. Now that I was forced to face the fact that they might be, I could barely breathe. I couldn't process what he had done to me or why, but deep down I'd suspected there was a reason for his actions.

A low rumble emanated from his chest at being challenged. Smith's hand shot out and clutched my upper arm, his nails digging into the tender skin as he shook me. "I don't give a damn about that. All that matters is that you're breathing. That I know no matter where we are and how much distance separates us that air is passing through those beautiful lips." He dropped his hold on me and took a step back, turning to face the window that looked out over Central Park. "You're strong, Belle. You are going to create a global empire. Someday you'll forget all about me."

"Is this why you brought me here?" I whispered, my voice brittle with the emotions building in me. "To break my heart again? Because I have news for you, there's nothing left to break. It's shattered—dust. Nothing will ever fix it."

Smith's eyes closed as he shook his head. His hand dropped to his side, breaking the electric connection sizzling between us. "I never wanted this for you. I tried to stay away."

"And you came for me anyway. Or am I just a line item to check off? Was it easier to export me across the Atlantic to do this?" It was a good thing we were in a suite the size of a house because I'd gone from whispering to screaming. The questions scratched my throat as I flung the accusations at him. The pain felt good—real—unlike the surreal nightmare that had trapped me.

"I don't know why you're here," he admitted, "or why I'm here. When I found out you were coming—"

"How did you find that out?" I interjected, crossing my arms as if they could afford me some amount of protection from what was happening.

"I have my sources."

The calmness of his answer made me want to chuck a lamp at him. "Sources? You mean *secrets*."

"Yes!" He rounded on me, stepping so close that the heat of his breath brushed over my face. One more inch and there would be no space left between us. "My secrets protect you. This is killing me. It would be easier to put a gun to my own head than walk away, but who will be there to protect you then?"

"I can protect myself," I said in a measured tone, forcing myself to ignore his closeness, even as a tight ache spread over my skin. One touch. I needed it. I needed one split second of contact to remember as I faced a lifetime of denial.

Which was why I kept myself frozen in place. Giving in wouldn't sate me. It would only make it harder.

"That's where you're wrong." Smith's head fell back as he drew a ragged breath. "Why did I fall in love with you?"

The world skidded to a stop, time slowing to a standstill as his words sunk in. I was still processing when he caught my waist and pulled me violently against him. His lips took even as they gave, reminding me that I belonged to him as he surrendered. All conscious thought fled me as

I tangled my fingers in his hair and held him to me. The fear vanished, but the anger remained and I bit into his lip until I tasted blood. Smith groaned, sweeping me off his feet as he smashed his mouth harder to mine and carried me toward the stairs. I had no idea where they led and I didn't care so long as I didn't have to let him go. I drew back, panting, when we reached the top step.

"You're mine," I breathed.

His eyebrows ratcheted up at my possessiveness, but a smile carved across his chiseled face. "In perpetuity."

"That sounds binding," I murmured, a giddy wave of hopeful fear overwhelming me. A moment ago, he'd tried to say goodbye to me. Now I was in his arms. I had no idea what came next.

"As your lawyer, I can assure you there is no escape clause." He pressed his forehead against me. "I can't stay away from you."

"Then don't," I suggested gently.

"I will protect you. You've given me your body, and I'll protect it with my own," he vowed.

"And what about my heart?" I placed a hand on his firm chest. "You carry it with you. Protect it?"

"With every breath I have left on this earth."

I wiggled from his grasp, landing lightly on the balls of my feet as he steadied me. Smoothing his necktie down, I inhaled deeply and released the fear and anger lingering in my core. My fingers closed over the silk, and I tugged gently on it as I led him through the door into a massive bedroom. Smith watched as I reached behind me and drew the zipper of my dress down, allowing the garment to flutter to the floor. I stood before him in my lacy garter and stockings. His jaw tightened as he loosened his tie, sending a pang of anticipation rolling across my exposed skin. My nipples hardened into points, struggling against the lace holding them captive. Smith tossed the tie to the floor and adjusted his erection as his face darkened with the dominance that consumed me.

"Show me," I commanded him, emboldened by his swift, physical reaction. "Show me you belong to me."

His eyes flashed, but he didn't protest. This wasn't how the game was played. Instead he crossed to me, stripping off his shirt and abandoning it. I braced for his hands—for the rough and unyielding brutality with which he always took me, but he dropped to his knees before me. His hands crossed in supplication before him.

He was giving me control. I bit my lip as he carefully plucked the satin gripping my stockings until my garter no longer held them, then he hooked his fingers around the band of my panties and drew them slowly to my feet. He waited as I stepped out of them and widened my stance, granting him access to my sex. Smith's mouth brushed over the smooth skin of my belly, trailing lower until his mouth closed hungrily over my pussy. He didn't use his hands, rather he planted them on the floor as the warm, moist tip of his tongue flicked along my seam, spreading me open. He worshipped me like this, on his hands and knees, his tongue stroking patiently until the first moan spilled from my mouth. He forced his tongue into my hole, circling my swollen entrance until my legs began to shake. I grabbed his hair to keep myself upright as he clamped his teeth gently over my clit and began to suck, urging the first trembling spasms of climax from me. But he didn't relinquish his position, instead he swirled his tongue languidly over my captured bud, freeing me from the agony of want to the numbing bliss of pleasure.

My knees buckled, and he held me upright without changing position. I wanted to collapse against him, needing the familiarity of his arms around me. Smith, however, appeared intent on a different means of comfort. He looked up to me, eyes burning, and waited for my next instruction. My fingers loosened my hold on his hair, but I didn't release him. Pulling softly, I guided him to his feet, still lost for words, and pointed to the bench at the foot of the bed before letting him go. He went to it and sat without a word.

"Take off your pants," I finally managed, my tone lacking the authority usually present in his demands, but he did as he was told anyway.

I studied him for a moment, my eyes lingering over the brutal lines of his arms and legs before they lighted upon the cock jutting up against the flat plane of his abdomen. My mouth watered at the sight, and I had to stop myself from crawling to him in offering. I was in charge, and I wasn't likely to get that opportunity again for while. Reaching behind me, I unhooked my bra and let it fall away. My stockings had rolled down slightly, but I didn't adjust them as I sauntered toward Smith, shamelessly swaying my ass.

"How does it feel to give me control?" I purred, tipping his chin up with my index finger.

"Different," he admitted with a smirk.

I tapped his cheek with my palm. "You're not the only one who can dole out punishments."

Smith crossed his hands behind his head and leaned back, giving me better access to his cock. "Punish away."

"I don't know if I'm punishing you or rewarding you," I said, playfully slapping his shaft.

"Keep doing it and I'll let you know," he advised.

But I had other plans for him. Straddling his lap, I dropped lower until my sex hovered teasingly over his crown. I rocked back and forth, lightly sweeping my slick seam over him. Smith's eyes closed as he groaned.

"A man only has so much patience, beautiful."

"I know you have better control than that," I said in a low voice even as I lowered farther, allowing his crest to breach my folds.

"I wouldn't count on it," he said gruffly. "I'm about a second away from flipping you over and spanking your petulant ass for being coy."

"I see. Is this what you want?" I nudged myself against his tip until he was barely inside me.

"Beautiful." His voice was thick with warning.

Now or never, I thought, knowing he wasn't joking about punishing me. There would be time for that later. The realization coiled through me, tightening across my muscles as I sank down, swallowing his shaft to the root. A slow grin spread across his face.

"That's it," he coaxed.

"How do you like being topped?" I murmured, brushing my lips over his.

"I could almost get used to it." He didn't move as I continued to roll my hips, seeking the perfect balance between depth and friction. He was so deep that it almost hurt—in the best possible way. I didn't ever want to get used to this delicious pain. I wanted to feel it each and every time we made love.

"Say it," I panted as I continued to writhe on his lap.

Smith's fingers found my nipples, pinching and toying with them until my breasts plumped, growing heavy with arousal. "Say what, beautiful? That your body was made for fucking? Or that I want you on my cock every day for the rest of my life?"

A strangled cry escaped me as I shook my head. I was so close—too close. All I needed to be pushed over the edge were three little words. The ones that I'd longed to hear since things had grown so complicated between us. He was everything I never knew I needed, and while that terrified me, I couldn't imagine a day without him either.

"I know," he soothed, wrapping an arm around my waist and drawing me closer. I melted into him as his hips began to thrust. He plunged into me with the precision of a man who understood exactly where a woman wanted to go and also how to get her there. "I know what you need to hear. I love you. Telling you is something I'm going to do every single day, beautiful."

"Oh God, I love you." I forced the words out as tingles turned into a wildfire, spreading white-hot through my limbs as his words burned across my heart. They'd branded me as his, imprinting across me like the molten tip of a knife. I was free and claimed. Liberated and bound. Smith Price owned me entirely.

Soft gasps turned to shuddering cries as I clung to him, wanting him deeper. I needed to be full of him, and as my taut muscles uncoiled around him, I moved harder and faster, lifting my ass and pushing back down even as my own climax diminished into subtle aftershocks that vibrated through my heavy sex. Smith grunted, jerking me down harder as he came, his eyes locking with me. The look we shared was raw and unguarded, each of us lowering our defenses.

His actions—his words—could kill me. I'd opened myself to him, exposed my weaknesses. But he'd shown me his as well. He'd taken my heart and transplanted it with his own.

Apart we were unguarded—defenseless to the outside world.

Together we were invincible.

elle slid onto the bed, collapsing into a boneless heap across the downy comforter. I studied her for a moment, trying to process what we'd both committed to. I'd brought her here out of selfishness, convinced I would be able to keep the situation under my control, but as always, she'd effectively destroyed my self-restraint on arrival.

That's what you wanted all along.

Now she was back in my bed. I'd almost managed to sell myself the lie that I could give her up. She looked up at me with her wary, cornflower blue eyes, and I knew she guessed what I was thinking. Reassurance was in order for both of us before we wound up shouting again. Sinking onto the bed, I beckoned for her to come closer. Whatever dominant streak had possessed her earlier was gone now, and she pushed herself swiftly into my waiting arms.

"This is where you belong," I murmured as I kissed the

top of her head, drinking in her comforting scent. I wouldn't deny that fact any longer.

"I never forgot that." The accusation was back in her voice. Whatever bliss I'd given her during our lovemaking session hadn't lasted.

"You have questions." I stated it as a fact. We'd given in to our emotions as soon as we saw one another. Now we needed to grapple with the larger issues that threatened to tear us apart.

"Only about a million." Her eyes flickered up to mine, and she stared me down.

"Ask and I will do my best to answer."

"Was the break-up staged?"

God, the woman could be a lawyer. She certainly knew how to go for the throat.

"Yes," I admitted. Her body tensed beside me, but I pulled her closer.

"By whom?"

There was that killer instinct again. Apparently she was going to let the fact that it involved Georgia Kincaid slide. For now. "I work for Hammond, but I also work for someone else."

"No shit, Sherlock," she retorted. "I figured that out a while ago."

But she hadn't figured out whom I worked for, or she wouldn't be asking me for that information now.

"Belle, I said I would do my best to answer, but I also need to protect you. That information is dangerous."

"You don't trust me." Her face fell as she spoke, and I resisted the urge to spill all of my secrets.

"I trust you, but I also love you. I have to weigh the possible consequences of you knowing too much."

"Fine," she huffed. "Was all of this a set-up? Do I even have a meeting tomorrow?"

"I'm a silent partner in Bless. I don't interfere. Your meeting with Abigail Summers is your business."

"And yours, too, it seems." This response was slightly less sarcastic. Progress. "Did you arrange for the meeting?"

I stared quizzically at her. It wasn't like her to show such a lack of confidence. She'd gone about starting Bless with the tenacity that had drawn me to her. Of course, I'd recently fucked with her perception of the world. The idea that I'd undermined her in any way left a bitter taste in my mouth. "You did that."

She relaxed a bit at this revelation.

"Beautiful, I gave you some money. That's where my contribution ended."

"Good." She snuggled against me, obviously pleased. "Speaking of money, how the hell does a lawyer afford a Bugatti and house the size of Harrods and a suite at the Plaza?"

I knew this question had preoccupied her for some time, and it wasn't the first time she'd hinted at wanting answers. More than once, she'd made offhand remarks about my wealth. "From my father. It's not a subject I like to discuss. I'm paid very well for solving questionable legal matters for my clients. But my wealth came from my father's life insurance policy. He left it all to me."

"How much was…" she trailed off, her eyes widening at her own rudeness.

"Ten million," I answered before she could feel too guilty.

"But, your house. Your car."

"It doesn't add up," I finished for her. "The house belonged to my family. My father purchased it not long after we moved from Scotland when he first started working for Hammond. It was an adventure to me at the time. It wasn't until I was an adult that I questioned exactly how he afforded it. Inflation hasn't risen that much." My joke fell flat in the tension hanging between us. "Now I know he must have done something truly heinous to receive such a reward from Hammond."

"Why do you keep it?" she asked softly as she placed her palm on my chest.

I clasped it tightly and shook my head. "I don't know. In a way it's a necessary reminder of what he's done to me and my family. To my parents. To Margot."

She tensed at the mention of my ex-wife.

"It reminds me of what I need to do," I said in reassurance, "not of her. The estate is like a chain around my neck. I can't free myself from it."

"Maybe you could take it off?"

"We both know it's not that simple." Belle carried a similar burden with her family estate.

"You're right. But even if you owned the house. That's not exactly an obscene amount of money."

"Are you saying that I'm worth an obscene amount of money?" I teased.

This time my light-hearted comment had the intended effect. "You are priceless."

She jerked up and smacked me quickly on the lips.

"You're getting us confused again." I brushed her hair back and felt my adoration for her multiply once more. "I was too young to take my inheritance, and as luck would have it, Hammond was the executor in charge of the funds."

"You call that lucky?"

"Not all luck is *good* luck. He invested it for me. God knows how much seedy information he used, but he turned it into a hundred million pounds before I was nineteen."

"A hundred million?" Belle repeated in shock. "And he just gave it to you?"

"Technically, it was mine, but yes. He did. It was play money to him. If he'd lost it all, it wouldn't have mattered. That he made that much didn't matter either. Although it did have the effect of winning me over. Suddenly, I owed him. So when he suggested I take up law at the university, I didn't refuse. It never even occurred to me that I had a choice."

"That's something I understand, too." The melancholy trace of obligation colored her words. "And by the time you started working for him, he owned you."

"You've heard this story before," I murmured, drawing her into my lap.

She blinked, her full lashes fluttering innocently over wise eyes. "Some parts were left out."

"I didn't like those chapters." I swallowed and looked away from her.

Belle's soft hand guided my face back to hers. "No good story lacks conflict. It made you the man you are."

"And what kind of man am I?"

She didn't shrink away at the harsh undercurrent in my voice.

"The kind of man I love," she answered simply.

"I am truly sorry for that."

This time her slap wasn't playful, and my hand shot out and caught her wrist in a tight squeeze. She pulled back, but I didn't relinquish control.

"Don't speak about the man I love that way," she ordered me.

"I don't take orders from you." But despite myself, I smiled. How this woman managed to turn my world upside down every time I was with her was beyond me. The fact that I liked it was even harder to grasp.

"This time you do," she said resolutely.

For a split second, I considered flipping her over and reminding her exactly who was in charge. Instead I shrugged. "Noted."

"That's all?" she countered. "You're not going to spank me?"

"Oh beautiful, I'm going to spank you. Hard. But I'm going to make you wait for it, because I think that's exactly what you want." She squirmed a little, rousing the attention of my cock, which had grown bored of the round of twenty questions. "I have other things in mind first."

"Oh yeah?"

I'd successfully steered her away from the unpleasant topics that had consumed the last hour of our lives.

"Lay across the bed. Feet over the side," I instructed her as I scooped her off my lap and deposited her back onto the sheets. Belle wiggled into place, and my gaze raked over the sight of her long legs still covered in silk stockings and the lace garter resting snugly across her belly. Reaching down, I unhooked it and drew it away before I shredded the hosiery from her.

"Those were expensive," she informed me.

"You really do want a spanking," I said gruffly, stroking my cock with my free hand as I appreciated my work. "I'll buy you more. But for now…"

I wadded the ruined stockings in my hand and held them to her mouth. She shot me a murderous look before she allowed me to stuff them in.

"You can't get yourself in more trouble if you can't talk, beautiful." I stroked my index finger along the plump curve of her lower lip. "Now stay."

My balls tightened as she held still. She was annoyed with me. That was clear. But she couldn't deny me either. The woman really was the perfect bottom. Submissive to a fault when I stripped her down and fiery as hell the rest of the time. Walking to the closet, I stopped and retrieved my tie from the floor. Then I pulled another one from a hanger. The two ties I'd asked her to choose between on her first day on the job. I'd given her a choice that day. She wasn't getting one now.

Returning to the bed, I lifted her leg, guiding her to bend it at the knee. Belle raised an eyebrow, but thanks to the makeshift gag, she couldn't question me as I took her wrist and brought it to her calf. I looped the silk tie tightly, binding her arm to her ankle, and ignored the muffled protest. Apparently, her obedience was a little out of practice.

"If you want me to stop, nod." I waited. But despite the frustrated look on her face, she stayed still and lifted the other leg. "That's what I thought."

I repeated the action. Stepping back, I surveyed my work, admiring the way the bindings put her cunt on display. In a few minutes, her muscles would begin to ache, but I had no doubt that she'd grow wetter with each passing second.

"I'll be right back." I swallowed a laugh as she shook her head and fought against my handiwork. "No."

Picking up the other stocking, I lifted her head and wrapped it around her mouth to prevent her from spitting out the gag. "Do you still want this?"

She stopped fighting and relaxed.

"Then be patient," I said before striding out of the room. I had what I needed already, but I took my time gathering it. Right now, she was probably trying to wriggle free, but only so she could pounce on me. The longer I waited, the more primed she would be. And I'd told her I had plans for her. In the end, my own impatience won out. Belle was still in the bed. She'd managed to scoot herself to the edge.

"Not the best idea," I told her as I set the champagne bucket and towel on the nightstand. "I don't want you bruising your ass before I get a chance to." Drawing out a cube, I held it over her chest, the heat of my hand sending droplets of icy water trickling over her breasts. Her nipples pebbled into beacons of want instantly, and I couldn't resist the urge to take them in my mouth. I sucked each one until I heard her moaning into the gag. Dropping the ice cube onto her navel, I straightened up and watched as it melted into a puddle on her belly before I took another from the bucket. I allowed this one to drip along her engorged sex, the water mixing with the slick proof of her arousal. Belle's eyes rolled back at the sensation, and I moved the remainder of the cube down, bringing it to the tight pucker on display. Her eyes flew open when it made contact, and this time she cried out. The sound made me want to shove my dick inside her, but I refrained, enjoying the little game too much for it to end so soon.

Belle loved being tied up. She got wet when I collared her. But nothing made her body respond more than promises, and I had a few to deliver.

"I'm going to fuck this," I told her, pushing the ice against the quivering hole. "And you are going to beg me to never stop."

She rocked against my hand, urging more contact, even as she looked like she was about to cry.

"It's okay," I soothed her. "I know you want it, beautiful, and I'll give it to you, but not tonight. You have no idea how much I want to right now, but you aren't ready. We're going to work on that. Is that okay?"

She nodded and I smiled. The ice was completely gone now, and I took another and placed it at the apex of her seam. "Don't move. If that ice falls, I'll have to stop."

Her body tensed, doing her best to comply as it slowly leaked down her slit. I drew my thumb across her pussy, coating it in the slippery arousal spilling from her and began to circle the tight entrance of her ass. "I love your ass. I want to fuck it and paddle it and worship it. You want that too, don't you?"

A choked sob escaped from her as she nodded again.

"Baby steps." I pushed against the snug rim until I was stroking her inside. "I can see your clit pulsing. It must be so hard to stay still, but you're doing so well. I love watching you fight your urges to give me control. It makes me so fucking hard." I pushed deeper and twisted to allow my other fingers to play with her cunt. Sliding my index finger into her weeping pussy, I found her g-spot and began to knead.

"You're going to come so hard for me in a minute, baby, and I want you to let go. You have no control, and I want to see you surrender to that. Can you do that?"

She didn't respond, but I felt her tightening around me. Quickly slipping another finger inside, I moved faster until I was fucking her relentlessly with my hand. Her thighs shook, and she arched up, fighting for balance that her bindings wouldn't afford. I pressed my other hand to her belly, anchoring her to the mattress as she transformed into a convulsing, sobbing wreck before my eyes. Her muscles gave way, too tired to fight any longer and the orgasm ripped through her, sending a gush of warm arousal onto my hand as she came. Then she went utterly still, save for the muscles quivering from the effort that came with being tied up. I withdrew from her slowly, savoring the way she continued to pulse against my fingers. Wiping off my hand with the towel, I then swept it gingerly over her sensitive pussy. Her head flopped from side to side to let me know it was too much, too soon.

"You're such a good girl," I murmured as I undid the ties and rubbed the indentations left on her flesh. "Good girls get to come like that. Are you going to continue to be good for me, beautiful?"

I took off the gag, and she breathed a yes, licking her dry lips.

"Wait right here." I stepped back and she shook her head. I *tsked*softly. "I'm going to draw you a bubble bath, and then I'm going to carry you to it. It might be a while before you can stand on your own two feet again."

"Yes, Sir," she whimpered as she lolled across the bed.

Fifteen minutes later, I scooped her limp body up and placed her in the bath. Belle relaxed into the water, her nipples grazing across the glassy surface. I corked the champagne I'd rescued from the bucket as she soaked. She jolted at the pop, but her eyes remained closed.

"Open your mouth, beautiful," I coaxed, sitting on the edge of the tub.

She obliged, her lips parting to reveal her white teeth. Slowly I drizzled champagne over her full lips, allowing it to trickle over her chin. It spilled across her collarbone, turning into a stream that ran between her perfect breasts.

"Seems like a waste of Dom Perignon," she murmured past the bubbles foaming over her tongue.

"I told you I was giving you a bubble bath." I emptied the bottle. I'd order another later. Another the night after that. I wanted to pamper her, treat her like the queen she was.

"Care to join me?" she asked shyly.

"That can be arranged."

Belle scooted forward, allowing me to slip in behind her. She melted against me as my arms coiled tightly around her torso, drawing her close. From now on, I wasn't letting her go.

"I wish it could always be like this." She sighed, releasing the wish as quickly as she'd stated it.

"Tonight it will be," I whispered in her ear.

"And tomorrow?" she pressed. "Can we pretend that this is our life?"

I heard what she was really asking: could we pretend the outside world didn't matter? I wanted to tell her we could—to promise the nightmare was over. But I'd lied to her before, and I was tired of it.

"Tonight it is."

"And tomorrow?" she asked again.

"Yes," I said, meaning it. Wanting it. "And every day it's in my power."

It wasn't enough. Not for either of us. But for one night, it could be.

# CHAPTER TWELVE

*T*he outfit was all wrong. The neckline was too low, dipping to the valley between my breasts. The skirt was too long. It fit me perfectly, as had every piece that had arrived courtesy of Smith's shopping excursion to Harrods, but it still wasn't right.

It wasn't sexy or daring or *enough*. I stared into the full-length mirror in the bathroom, trying to get a handle on exactly what was wrong. Given my company's title, a little black dress was exactly what I needed to wear to this afternoon's interview. But in New York, everyone wore them. I needed to stand out without drawing attention, and I had no idea how to do it.

"So much for becoming a fashion mogul," I muttered at my reflection.

"You're already a fashion icon," Smith said. He came up behind me and wrapped his arms around my waist. "Now what is the problem?"

"It's missing something. I have to impress this editor."

Just getting an interview wasn't going to ensure a coveted spot in her magazine. The thought set off a new wave of self-doubt. There were people who would kill to have this opportunity, and I was going to cock it up. Those people would have no problem walking into the *Trend* offices and wowing everyone with their poise.

God, if I couldn't nail a magazine article, how would I succeed in business?

"You are going to impress her." Smith spoke with an assurance that was typically male, but I shook my head.

"I have tried on every piece I brought."

"Wait here." His arms slipped away, and he disappeared back to the bedroom. When he returned, he held a pair of Louboutins. "These landed you your last job."

I took them, studying the leopard print. They were amongst my favorites, but I couldn't help worrying the print was cliché. I was definitely overthinking things now.

Smith seemed to sense my reluctance. Dropping to one knee, he reached for the shoes. Then he reverently slid them onto my feet. "You walked in to my office in these shoes, and I knew right then and there, you were different. Here was this gorgeous woman. She was polished and professional. I wanted to fuck you on the spot."

"I'm not sure that's what I should be going for," I said dryly.

"That was my response," he said as he stood and took my shoulders. Spinning me around, his eyes met mine in the mirror. "I responded that way because I knew you were a woman who knew what she wanted."

"I wanted a job," I murmured.

"And you got it."

I'd also received him in the bargain. Maybe he was on to something. I studied myself more closely. The black dress, which had felt ordinary moments before, had transformed with Smith's addition. Suddenly I wasn't average. I was bold and commanding. I straightened up, a smile creeping across my face.

"These must be lucky," I said at last.

"That's not it." He shook his head and pulled me against his hard body. "They're simply a representation of who you are. Sexy, sophisticated. A woman that doesn't have to try to draw the attention of everyone in the room."

"You're pretty good at this," I teased. "Do you want a job?"

"I don't think I could handle working under you, beautiful. I'm far too fond of being on top."

Of me. Of the world. Of everything he touched. A tingle danced down my spine. I'd gotten his attention and somehow I'd kept it.

"It's time you stop second-guessing yourself and you start listening to the truth," he continued.

"Are you going to go all alpha on me outside the bedroom?"

"If that's what it takes," he warned me lightly. "But I'm not going to have to, because you already know all of this. You just have to believe it."

I dropped my head to his shoulder. "Now I know why I fell in love with you."

"Were you doubtful before?" He grinned wickedly, pressing his lips to a spot behind my ear.

"I've had my moments." I turned into him, tipping my chin to drink in his handsome face. When we were together like this, it was easier to see how it had happened despite how hard I'd fought to keep him at a distance. I had questioned why I fell in love with him. Hell, I'd worried about my sanity. But since the moment I'd realized I'd fallen, I'd known I loved him. Now, how and why didn't seem important. Not so long as we could stick together.

"You are going to have them eating out of your hand," he promised me.

"How do you know that?"

"Because you've had me eating of your hand since the day we met," he explained. Then he sealed his confession with a lingering kiss that left no room for doubt.


THE EDITORIAL OFFICE of *Trend* was housed in a building every bit as imposing as the bustling streets of New York. My eyes traveled up, trying to take in the full glory that was home to the oldest and most important fashion magazine in the world. As if on cue, my mobile buzzed.

"Are you there?" Lola asked when I answered.

I cradled the phone closely, pressing my index finger to my other ear to block the street noise. "I'm here. Remind me why you aren't?"

"Because I have to finish this bloody portfolio. Remember, talk like we're already a huge success," she advised.

"That would be easier if we had so much as a website," I

muttered, my stomach flipping over as I stared at the revolving door in front of me.

"It went live two hours ago."

"What?" I squealed. "Are you some type of witch?"

"That's bitch," she corrected me. "We're open by invitation only. Now go in there and wow Abigail Summers."

We hung up, and I strode into the lobby of Dwyer Publishing. If I had the time, I probably would have been intimidated by the polished marble floors and or the oversized screens displaying recent magazine covers. But a freak out was not on the schedule. Instead I headed toward a the lifts.

"Floor?" An attendant asked as I stepped inside.

"Twenty-five."

"Very good." He pushed the button and then returned to a practiced position.

I stared at the old man and his pressed uniform, wondering how long he'd done this job. He'd probably delivered many a hopeful fashionista to that floor. I had half a mind to bombard him with questions.

"You'll do fine," he said kindly as the lift shuddered to a stop.

I managed a nervous smile. The doors slid open and I came face to face with a pretty redhead. Light freckles dusted her porcelain complexion, and, perhaps knowing basic black would only wash her out, she wore a brilliant, emerald green shirt dress.

She stuck her hand out. "Katherine Harper. Abigail's assistant. Can I just say we're so excited about the Bless concept?"

"Th-thank you," I stammered.

"Can I get you anything? A coffee? Water?" She paused, screwing up her face in an effort to recall more options. "Oh, tea?"

"I'm fine," I assured her. Given the way I was shaking, I'd probably spill it all over myself.

"Are you ready to go straight into the interview or would you like a moment?" She continued leading me through the maze of cubicles toward a large corner office.

"I'm ready." That was a lie, but I pasted my smile on.

Katherine waved as we passed a desk. "That's Nolan. He's our international editor. We've borrowed him from France for a few weeks."

Nolan tipped his head, not bothering to look up from his tablet.

"He thinks we're all crass and overweight," she whispered when we were out of earshot.

Judging from that acknowledgment, I'd sensed he had the typical French attitude toward Americans. At least I didn't have to interview with him.

Katherine seemed immune to his attitude, however. She'd dismissed him as easily as he had dismissed her. "We're so eager to hear all about Bless and where you came up with the concept."

Was this what it was like to be wined and dined—in the business sense?

Katherine froze in her tracks and spun around. Her overly cheerful demeanor was replaced by a conspiratorial whisper. "This is pretty overwhelming, isn't it? The first time I walked in here, I thought I was going to throw up."

"I still might," I admitted with a grateful smile.

"Look, Belle, you have a great idea. When I read your partner's pitch, I was sold, and trust me, there are a lot of women who need this service, myself included. Do you know how hard it is to afford to keep up with my own job? I have to come to work in the latest pieces." Her voice continued to lower as she spoke. I could tell it wasn't something she shared lightly. I'd only been in New York for a day, and I already felt like I couldn't keep up with it.

I took a deep, steadying breath. I was here for a reason. The business plan I'd finished over the weekend was solid. Lola's publicity and marketing plan was incredible. We even had the money to fund our launch. Standing in front of me was our first target customer, and she was already sold. Things were in place. "Thanks. I needed to hear that."

"Believe me, my credit cards thank you." She squared her shoulders, her eyes widening in excitement. "Ready?"

"Yes." This time I meant it.

Considering the powerhouse impression I had of Abigail Summers, I was surprised to come face to face with a petite brunette whose hair was piled messily on top of her head. A pair of Versace reading glasses perched on her long nose. Only someone as powerful as the editor of *Trend* could command respect without doing her hair in the morning. She glanced up from her desk long enough to appraise me disinterestedly before turning her attention back to her file.

"This one." She held out a piece of paper, and Katherine scurried to grab it.

"Your appointment is here," Katherine interjected as her boss continued to sort through papers.

"Is she?" she asked, her voice flat as her gaze fixed on me. "Thank God, you're here. Call the doctor, I think I need a new prescription."

Apparently she was a little sarcastic and a lot bitchy. Katherine's eyes darted from me to the desk and back again, softening apologetically at the edges. Annoyance stirred in my chest. I'd dealt with plenty of people like Abigail before. I'd even worked for a man just like her, and if my experience with Smith had taught me anything, it was that people like that only responded to strength.

"Belle Stuart." I stepped toward her desk and stuck out my hand. "It's a pleasure to meet you, Abigail."

So much for staying safely in ass-kissing territory. Arrogance appreciated flattery, but it respected confidence, and respect yielded more between two parties. At least that was what I told myself.

I could also have just totally screwed myself.

Abigail snatched her reading glasses off and tossed them on her desk, rubbing her temple before gesturing for me to take a seat. "Kat, grab us some coffee."

Maybe I'd made the right call, although I decided against telling her that I preferred tea.

"Belle, is it?" Abigail said as soon as her assistant had left the room. "Tell me why you're here again."

I knew exactly why I was here. I'd been going over my talking points for days. Lola had grilled me over them before I'd flown out. The fact that she had no idea why I was in her office was what was tough to swallow.

My eyes locked with hers, and I paused to consider my answer, and that's when I saw it. A slight flicker glinting ominously. Her face was otherwise unreadable. But that was all the information I needed. She knew why I was here. "Your magazine wants to do an editorial on my start-up," I said in a sugary tone. There was no need to call her on her deception. Abigail Summers was either testing me or punishing me. Either way, I had a good feeling of where I stood with her.

"Let's cut to the chase, shall we?" She folded her hands on her desk and waited for me to respond. I nodded. "We're both busy women, so I see no reason to pretend otherwise. I told Katherine she could do these little pieces because she's concerned about the magazine's image. Or rather, my image. I don't really give a fuck what people think about me."

"I find that refreshing," I said sincerely.

"Then I hope you won't be offended when I tell you that I don't care about a start-up company unless they're cloning Michael Fassbender. No offense."

My eyebrows raised as I pressed my mouth into a thin line. Oh, I was offended. Mostly because her message was pretty clear. "So *Trend* isn't doing a series on female entrepreneurs?"

"It is," Abigail said, "but I'm not. Frankly, this meeting is a waste of my energy."

"Frankly," I said as I stood back up and smiled down at her, "I feel the same way. I'll show myself out."

Katherine met me at the doorway. "Is everything okay?"

"The interview is over," I told her, "and I was leaving."

She sucked in a breath as she shook her head. "I'll be handling the interview personally. I just wanted you to meet my editor."

Too little. Too late. I'd met her brilliant editor, and I was smart enough to know that I'd been dragged into some type of internal power struggle. I dealt with enough of that in my personal life.

"Belle," Abigail called, "I'm sure you're a bright woman with vision and promise but *Trend* isn't about spotlighting potential. It's a showcase."

I should let it go. The best course of action was to nod and walk away. There was very little potential for fall-out in that scenario. But it was pretty clear there was very little possibility that *Trend* was going to be featuring my company. "A showcase whose subscription sales are down over twenty percent in the last year. Your magazine has also cut print runs to less than half of what they were five years ago even though digital magazines only account for 10% of your sales. Not to mention that you're actively courting advertisers for the first time in twenty years, because they're no longer coming to you. Showcase whatever you want. You're the editor. But take it from someone whose business is in the growth stage, you need to worry a little less about your traditions and a little more about your relevance."

Her face remained impassive as I dumped this on her. Abigail picked up her glasses and slipped them back on. "Enjoy your time in New York."

I'd been dismissed. It wasn't the first time, but it was the time that carried the most heartbreak. I'd invested my dream in today, and it had all been a sham. Bless still felt vulnerable to me, as if one wrong move would kill the whole deal.

And I'd just made the wrong fucking move.

I didn't bother to return Abigail's pleasantry; instead I walked out, leaving a dazed Katherine behind me. I'd just passed Nolan's cubicle, wondering if being a wanker was a prerequisite to work here, when she caught up with me.

"I'm so, so sorry," she said breathlessly. "I have no idea what that was about."

I spun around, trying to keep my frustration in check. Katherine had been kind to me from minute one. This wasn't her fault. But since she was the only one around, she was going to bear my rage. "It was about control. She's in control of this magazine."

*And you're not*, I added silently. I had no idea what was going on between Katherine and her boss, but I had a pretty good idea that neither of them particularly liked one another. It was obvious that Abigail didn't care for her or her ideas.

"She was the one who okayed the idea." A defensive current ran through Katherine's words. "She specifically chose you."

"And she unchose me." I felt a little calmer now. "Katherine, don't worry about it. I'm not interested in being a pity piece. In a few years, she won't be able to ignore me or my company, but I'll be more than happy to ignore her."

Katherine's lips twitched, but she kept the smile off her face. "I'd appreciate that."

"Something told me that you might." The down button on the lift dinged as its doors slid open. "Good luck."

"I'd say the same to you, but I don't think you're going to need it. Not with your attitude."

"Thank you," I said as I stepped inside. "For your words earlier and for the chance to come here."

"I'm not certain you should be thanking me for that." She laughed but it sounded hollow.

I held the door open with my arm. "No, you showed me earlier that I belong here. I belong in your magazine."

"I wish it was my magazine."

"It was your idea to reinvent its image, and it's a good one," I assured her. "But I think right now we're both in the wrong place. I'm going to take this lift and get back to where I'm supposed to be."

"If only I knew where I was supposed to go." Her tone grew wistful.

"You'll figure it out, and when you do, give me a call. The world needs us promising women to stick together."

Katherine leaned in and pecked me on the cheek. "You're right. Now if you'll excuse me, I have to stay here and do my time."

As the lift carried me to the lobby, I considered what Abigail had said. By the time I reached the ground floor, all my anxiety had vanished. This terrifying, life-changing meeting had been nothing but a blip. So *Trend* wouldn't be catapulting my company into super stardom? I could do that on my own.

I dialed Lola, worried that she'd finally fallen asleep, but she answered immediately. "How did it go?"

"Abigail Summers told me that *Trend* wasn't interested in potential, so I rattled off those figures you gave me on the magazine's subscription issues."

"And then what?" Lola was breathless on the other end.

"She told me to enjoy my trip and went back to work." I glided through the revolving door and found myself back in front of the Dwyer building. This time it didn't feel so imposing.

"You scared the most successful woman in fashion." Lola paused. "You're on your way."

"So you aren't mad?" I asked with relief.

"Not at all. There was no way we could launch in that publication timeframe. We aren't ready!"

I froze in my tracks. "Then why am I here?"

"I wanted to scare the future most successful woman in fashion," she teased. "I sent you because now you've faced your biggest rejection. How do you feel?"

"Like proving her wrong," I answered automatically.

"And you're going to."

Yes, yes, I was.

# CHAPTER THIRTEEN

*T*he room was utterly still, its furnishings and lighting carefully chosen to blanch color from the room. Walking into the old, and very off Broadway, theatre had the effect of stepping into a vintage postcard. The whole place belonged to a different place and time, even the actors who quietly made their way onto the stage as an antique grandfather clock struck the hour. The two actors unrobed and began to dance in a slow, haunting rhythm. Their movements mirrored one another's and as they're hands finally met, they arched backwards writhing as the song's tempo sped up. But despite how their bodies smashed against one another, they remained separate— two forces of motion colliding but never combining. It was a fight for control.

They had no audience save one beautiful older woman. The lurkers would arrive at dusk for their vicarious thrills.

The Looking Glass was a macabre floorshow, a spectacle of sensual burlesque that managed to unnerve and incite at the same time. I approached the woman watching silently at the bar. She didn't look up as I came nearer, didn't demand to know how I'd managed to get into the closed theatre. Her eyes remained glued to the conflict on stage, her auburn hair cascading down her shoulder and blocking me from studying her once familiar face.

"Mistress Alice," I greeted her in a low voice. That was what she was known by here—the moniker she'd given herself when she concocted her theatre of dreams—but that wasn't her real name. Very few people in New York knew that. In fact, I currently might have been the only one.

She didn't look to me, although her lips curved into a slight smile. "You're on the wrong continent."

"But am I in the wrong place?" We'd seen each other through the years on my occasional trips to the States for business or pleasure. This was the second time she was my business.

"I doubt that, Smith." She stood, her silk robe fluttering gracefully closed over her long legs and gestured toward the rear corridor.

Age had made her lovelier and distance had made her softer. The lines of her elegant face had sharpened even as her smile had grown kinder. She'd only had to put an ocean between her past and herself. It hadn't been a desperate choice. It had been a calculated one.

"How is Georgia?" she asked as she softly closed the door to her private dressing room.

I swallowed. Of course that would be the first person

she asked about. "She's well." I didn't elaborate further at this point. "How are you, Samantha?"

"Business is thriving." It wasn't an answer.

I raised an eyebrow.

"I'm lonely," she admitted. "My children insist on staying in London and my lovers tire quickly."

It was a more direct answer than I'd expected, but then again, Samantha had never felt the need to engage in the perverse mind games her husband was so fond of.

"And Hammond?" she asked dutifully.

"Complicated." I chose the word carefully. She was, in point of law, still married to him. Although she'd put an ocean between them nearly ten years ago.

"Everything with my husband is complicated." Her voice was brittle, coated in regret and self-recrimination. "And you and your sister still work for him?"

"Yes, we do." Now we were coming to the point. Samantha had always considered Georgia and I her adopted children, and in reality, she'd been the nearest thing to a mother I'd had for a very long time. Even as my own mother faded from this earth, she was there. She'd tried to protect us when she realized that the intentions of her husband were far from paternally motivated. But, in the end, she'd ran as we all did. She'd been the only one to ever successfully do it.

Her eyes snapped shut and when they opened they flashed. "She should have stayed."

"I shouldn't have taken her back." It was the closest I'd ever come to apologizing for my naivety.

"You were young." Samantha dismissed my confession.

"God knows what Hammond told you was happening to her here."

He had sold me lies and I had swallowed them, choosing to believe that I was the hero sent to deliver my helpless sister from the dangerous chameleon that had deceived us all. I'd flown to New York and lured her home, delivering her into the hands of the true predator.

"In so many ways I broke her as much as he did," I said softly, recalling how readily she'd sank to her knees at Velvet before the cane.

"She's not broken. It would be a mistake to ignore the obvious fact that she is naturally submissive," Samantha advised. "Despite that, his actions were unforgivable."

"You took her for a reason and it never occurred to me to consider that."

"Have you ever considered that she wanted to go back?" Samantha asked in a soft voice that highlighted the trace of Scottish burr that we both shared.

Yes. I had come to understand that Georgia had chosen to return to England and to Hammond's bed. Just as she had chosen to continue this charade. But with age had come a rationality that had saved her, in part, from herself. There was an intentionality to her decisions that had been absent then. "She was too young to make that choice."

"But now she's made another?" Samantha guessed. "Or have you come to see my show and play?"

"Both, I suppose. If you have tickets available."

"For you and?" She trailed away, the question hanging in the air between us.

"A woman."

"That I suspected," she said dryly.

"And yet you asked," I countered. "My girlfriend is with me on this trip."

"She must be important to bring her here—or perhaps she is understanding?"

"We'll come for the show." My message was clear. Belle could appreciate Samantha's delicate, provocative theatre, but I wasn't about to descend with her to Wonderland, not after what had happened with Velvet.

"It's a pity that you two don't see eye to eye on such matters."

I hadn't come to explain the intricacies of my sex life with her. "I'm afraid there's a bit more to it than that."

"You'll bring her then. I'd like to meet the woman who captured your interest so entirely."

"Perhaps." Given what we had to discuss it was possible her invitation would be rescinded. Time and distance might undermine the sense of betrayal she'd once felt. She had remained married to Hammond through the years.

"I suppose there's no sense avoiding this business any longer." Her arm stretched toward a weathered side table for a crystal decanter. Samantha poured us each a drink.

"You still have a penchant for gin." I set my glass to the side.

"I see you don't."

The truth was I didn't have the stomach for drinking today. "There's been some developments at home."

Samantha downed her drink in one long swig. "And you're here to do what exactly? Drag me home or warn me to stay put?"

"I'm here as a courtesy."

"To whom?" she asked.

"To you." This was my calculated risk. Telling Samantha was a gamble, because her loyalty to Hammond was questionable. To my knowledge the two hadn't spoken for years but they also hadn't divorced.

"I have a feeling I'm going to need another drink." She filled her glass again but she didn't gulp it down. Instead she caressed the rim with her index finger, her eyes staring straight through me to a place beyond this room.

"Hammond is under investigation." The trick to cluing her in was to only give herself enough warning to prepare her own affairs.

"Does he know this?"

It was the one question I'd hoped she wouldn't ask. If I lied and said he did, I ran the risk of her innocently revealing it to him. If I told her the truth, I gave her the rope to hang me.

Samantha's head tilted so that her gaze refocused on me. "You don't have to answer that."

My silence already had, and my hesitation had told her something else.

"I don't blame you," she said after a few moments of heavy silence. "He's done unforgivable things...."

"But?" I sensed the qualification without her making the excuse for him.

"No but." She smiled wanly and took a drink. It slid down her throat with an audible gulp. "As his lawyer you know we're still married. What happens if...if he's arrested? Am I in danger?"

"There's no longer an *if*, Samantha. The arrest is coming."

She didn't ask how I knew that. She'd already guessed I had a role in what was to come. "Will I be extradited?"

"That's highly unlikely."

"But not impossible." She didn't wait for me to answer. "It's no matter. My affairs have been separate from his for years."

"That was a judicious move," I reassured her. It was entirely possible that she would be sought out by the courts, but more than likely as a witness against her husband's crimes. That she had fled the country so many years before indicated that she too feared his reach. But giving the mounting evidence we'd collected and turned over to the authorities, her testimony was mostly unnecessary.

There was little more I could do to reassure her. I'd accomplished what I came to do. "I should be going. I'm certain you have things to attend to before this evening's performance."

"I appreciate you coming here to warn me," Samantha said as she walked me leisurely toward the door. "It's best not be caught off-guard by hearing it from the paper, I suppose."

"You did your best to protect us. You tried to help Georgia." I lowered my voice. "You genuinely cared when so few people did."

Samantha took my chin in her papery hand and studied me before sighing. "But did I do enough?"

"You did more than anyone else." I wrapped my arms

around her lithe frame and hugged her tightly. She had tried and although I'd once blamed her for abandoning us. I understood now. Some choices were between life and death. Living with Hammond—living with his toxic deceit —was a slow death. I couldn't begrudge her flight from that agony.

"Bring this woman to my show." Samantha's eyes narrowed into slits as she poked a finger into my chest. This time it was an order. "I'd like to meet her and perhaps you'll show her other things as well."

I clenched my jaw, trying to hold back what could be misinterpreted as an insult. "She struggled with Velvet."

"Velvet has its own ghosts," she said wisely. "You're unmatched there. You have too much history with that place."

She was right. There could never be a true exchange of power there. Not while I clung so tightly to my control whenever I entered its door.

"I'll consider it," I reiterated, still unwilling to commit.

"Don't hide who you are from her, Smith." The sharp edge of warning ran through her words.

"She's seen the beast inside me." I spoke so softly I wasn't certain she could hear me.

"There is no beast," Samantha admonished, ruffling my hair. "Only a man."

I wanted to believe her, but she saw me through a mother's eyes, and although she had some sense of the depths of my depravity, our relationship had never crossed the lines that Hammond's had with Georgia. "If only that were true."

"All humans are creatures subject to our basest needs."

I didn't bother to correct her again. I'd given Belle a choice. I'd hinted at who I was. I'd given her a taste. She'd chosen to stay with me. She'd also chosen to walk away. The woman was subject to nothing. She was the one in control. That made her the only light shining in the darkness of my world.

It made her the only one capable of saving my soul.

# CHAPTER FOURTEEN

*J* wandered the streets for a few hours as I contemplated my next move. Decisions had to be made. When I finally returned to the hotel, I nearly stumbled on the leopard print heels that had been left in the entry. She'd made it as far as the suite's dining room table. I watched her from the doorway, not wanting to disturb her as she worked. The purple glow of twilight lit across her fair features, turning her porcelain complexion rosy. Belle was always lovely, but today haloed in the late afternoon light she looked like an angel—a fucking brilliant, sexy as sin angel. Her brows knitted together as she typed furiously. Withdrawing my mobile I snapped a photo of the unguarded moment. The shutter sound broke her concentration and she glanced up, a smile spreading slowly across her face.

"I hope you got my good side," she muttered in mock annoyance.

I laughed as I selected the picture and set it as my mobile background. "They're all good sides."

"You're too easy on me." She leaned back in her seat, revealing more notes strewn around her.

That was because being with her was easy. It hadn't always been. Not when we had been caught up in trying to deny our attraction to one another. Since we'd given in the outside world had gotten more complicated but us—the us that existed in private—was simple.

"How was your meeting?" I crossed to her and began to knead her shoulders. Belle shifted back, allowing me a glimpse of her pale, creamy throat.

She sighed before answering in a tired voice, "Terrible."

"Oh?" I had to restrain myself from loosing my temper. The idea that things had gone poorly—that she was upset—lit a slow, simmering rage at my core.

"It doesn't matter." Her hand caught mine and squeezed, instantly soothing the fury building inside me. "I don't know what I expected, but the editor was a bitch."

I made a mental note to look into this editor. "I'm sorry."

It was the most comfort I could offer at the moment.

"I'm over it. Really," she said when I shot her a dubious look.

"Dinner?" I said. I didn't believe for one second that she'd written off whatever had transpired this afternoon. Perhaps a little wine would ease the story out of her.

She bit her lip, glancing quickly to her laptop. "I have a few more emails to return."

"Isn't the lawyer supposed to be the workaholic?"

"I know, right?" She pulled gently out of my grasp. "Give me an hour?"

"That will be perfect, beautiful." I pressed a kiss to her forehead before excusing myself to attend my own business. An hour would also give me time to prepare for the evening.

Georgia didn't answer her private line, not shocking given the time difference between London and New York. No doubt she was preoccupied with matters at the club. I'd seen to most of my other affairs before I'd left which gave me to time to arrange dinner. An hour later, I pried Belle from her work and led her onto the suite's private terrace with my hands clapped over her eyes. Only a pink sliver of sunset remained over the horizon. The city was covered in a dusky haze that sketched buildings into shapes and the trees of Central Park into bare limbs against the twinkling lights of distant skyscrapers. Autumn in New York was a magical time, when the bustling city contracted in preparation for winter.

I released her when we reached the table that Geoffrey had set up in the middle of the patio. A half dozen candles illuminated the simple spread of pasta I'd asked him to procure from Garazzo's, one of the few establishments that had survived since the first time I'd visited the ever-changing metropolis. There was a certain elegant rustic quality to classic Italian home cooking, and Belle's gasp of delight rewarded the effort I'd put into arranging the dinner.

I pulled out the chair, my hand remaining on its back until her napkin was tucked into her lap.

"This looks amazing," she said, ladling a massive helping of pasta onto her plate. "I just realized I skipped lunch."

"So your meeting was terrible but you still felt the need to work all afternoon?" I couldn't quite figure out if she was working through disappointment or trying to keep herself busy to avoid feeling it.

"It was," she admitted. She swirled her fork around the noodles and took a large bite.

"I'd like to hear about it."

She paused as if to consider my request before she related the events of her interview with Abigail Summers. When she finished I was barely controlling the seething anger about to boil over.

"You're mad," she noted when she finally finished.

"It was disrespectful," I said in a low voice. I could think of a few more choice terms to describe Summers's behavior but I kept them to myself. I

"Yes," she said, "but Abigail Summers gets to be disrespectful. Honestly, I'm over it."

"You?" I repeated pointedly.

"Apparently," she said, dropping her napkin onto the table and creeping over to my lap, "I deal quite well with rejection these days."

"Don't look at me, beautiful. I'm not about to test your theory." My arms circled around her trim waist. "I only want you closer."

We stayed like that under a black painted sky. The noise of the city dying away until the only sound I processed was her faint breathy inhalations.

"Up here you can almost see the stars." She gazed into the darkness, searching for their glittering presence. "It was one of my favorite things about my family's estate."

She spoke of her family home as if it was already lost. I knew otherwise, although I'd chosen not to get involved until she asked me—or the situation became dire.

"I hardly remember the stars," I admitted.

"We should go somewhere quiet where they aren't hidden by the city," she murmured.

"Of course, beautiful."

"I want it to be like this forever," she whispered. "Just us."

*Us.* The subject had been on my mind perpetually since she had arrived in my suite yesterday. If I was being honest I'd thinking about us since long before then. Here, high above the chaotic city, we seemed possible once more. I hadn't been able to figure out how to make it work in London. I had forced her to face me so that I could explain. My orchestrated betrayal had burrowed like a deeply imbedded thorn, and I'd been certain that the only way to remove it was to tell her the truth. Or as much of it as I dared to share. "We could if we stayed here, beautiful."

She laughed lightly but the bell-like sound ceased when her eyes met mine. "You're serious?"

"Why wouldn't I be?" I asked her. "You're the only thing tying me to London and now you're here."

Belle tilted her gorgeous face up to stare at me. I already knew here answer. "I have a life in London."

"I know. I wan't serious," I said dismissively.

"You were serious," she said, her voice growing softer as

she continued, "I wish I could be, too, but I have Clara and the new baby. My aunt. Edward."

I had to remind myself that the ties that bound her to London weren't the shackles that held me captive. Belle had people that she loved, something that I didn't, holding her there. Each name she spoke was a reminder that I wasn't her entire world.

"You look jealous," she accused.

"You can't blame me for wanting you all to myself." She could, in fact. It was selfish and short-sided. Those people had made her who she was, transforming her into the woman I loved, and if I could, I would take her away from all of them. Samantha had been wrong. I was a beast, a primitive creature that knew nothing beyond my own wants. And right now, I would trap Belle if I could. Back her into a corner. Scare her into staying. And not an ounce of me felt guilty for that.

"You're going to have to learn to share," she teased, trailing her index finger across my palm.

"I don't share, beautiful," I reminded her. "You belong to me."

This silenced her. When she finally spoke, her words came out in halting and half-formed. "I do. But...Smith, I want....more."

"More that me?" I swallowed hard on this revelation.

"Yes, and no," she tacked on swiftly. "If I have to choose, I'll choose you. Every time. At any cost. I just wish it wasn't the case."

"I do, too, beautiful."

This time I spotted the slide of her throat. "Then we'll

move to New York. It would be good for Bless."

She was willing to give it all up. Uproot her existence and fore sake all others. It was what I needed to know. "No," I said firmly. "Birds of a feather, remember?"

"I don't want to go home if its going to be dangerous for you," she murmured, finally giving words to the fear that had driven her to such a desperate agreement.

How could I tell her that I wanted to keep her here for that reason? That returning to London together was akin to painting a bullseye on her back? "I don't want to give you up."

The thoughtless words slipped from my mouth and lodged between us.

"What happened to facing the storm together?"

I turned away from her, searching for her answer in the dark, moonless night. She grabbed my face, her nails digging into my jaw.

"Don't you dare." A hysterical edge seeped into her voice. "You were right. I can live without you, but I don't want to. I am strong, but I'm stronger with you. We're stronger."

But we aren't invincible. I kept the thought to myself. "I'm stronger with you, too."

And yet, she was my greatest weakness. She had made me vulnerable. If Hammond made a move, if he placed stock in suspicion, it was no longer a simple matter of killing me.

"Then don't ever say that again." She blinked and tears cascaded down her face. "Don't ever fucking saying that."

I swiped them away with the pad of my thumb.

"I won't."

"Sometimes you can be such a bloody wanker," she said with a sniffle.

"And still you love me," I teased.

"No one ever accused me of having good judgment." Her lips curled at the corners.

This was how I wanted to spend this time with her. Trials awaited us in London and, sooner than I would like, we would have to face them. "We only have a few days. Let's enjoy them. Pretend that we're on a holiday and we have nothing but a blissful, simple life ahead of us full of sex and success and..."

"And?" she prompted, willingly joining me in my game. "What else do we have in this ideal life?"

I brushed a finger along her chin. "I don't know. If we're playing pretend, I suppose we could have anything we wanted."

"If only." Belle's eyes fluttered down, her cheeks darkening.

"If only what?" I pressed. "What do you want, beautiful? Let me give it to you. Maybe not today or tomorrow. But someday. Let's keep ourselves focused on someday."

"I don't know. It's...silly. I don't even know what I was thinking exactly."

I understood. Belle was a woman—an ambitious woman—but that didn't mean she'd given up on more domestic pursuits. "A ring?" I guessed.

"Someday," she repeated softly. "I know it's a long way off. I'm not ready either. I just..."

"What else?" I asked, ignoring her insecurity. "A baby?"

Her eyes widened. "You don't...um..."

"I don't seem the type. I know, but I'll let you in on a secret. People change, beautiful." I kissed her softly. "You changed me."

Never mind that all of this was a fantasy. For a moment I needed to pretend it was possible, because she deserved that much. If she was willing to give up everything for me, I wanted her to know that I would do everything in my power to give her a full life.

"Are you saying you want a baby?" she asked, her eyes narrowing suspiciously. "Or are you trying to get in my knickers?"

"I'm always trying to get in your knickers." I slid a hand down her belly and pushed it between her thighs. "A baby is a while off, but I wouldn't mind the practice."

"How generous of you." The dryness of the comment was undercut by her sharp intake of breath as I rubbed her sex through her dress's silky fabric.

"I can be *very generous*." My thumb began to circle, using the material for added friction. "Even when you're fully clothed, I can't keep my fucking hands off you. It feels good, doesn't it? Having your panties scratching over your clit? Are they wet yet, beautiful?"

I already knew the answer. Her dress had grown damp as I continued to manipulate her pussy through her clothes.

"Yes," she moaned.

"I can feel it." I captured her mouth and kissed her deeply. When I broke away, she was trembling. "We should get you out of these clothes."

Hooking an arm around her, I guided her onto her feet. My fingers found the zipper hidden under her arm and I slid it down slowly as I continued to kiss her. "You're mine, aren't you?" I asked. "Do you want me to claim you for all of New York to see?"

We were far too high up to risk casual sightings from the street, and the seclusion of our suite's terrace afforded a great deal of privacy. I had no desire to share Belle or her body with anyone else. Still there was no way to discount any voyeurism.

Her breath sped up and she bit her lip before nodding.

"You're so dirty." I continued to strip her until she standing naked in the crisp, evening air. Her nipple were sharp points, and although she shivered, she didn't complain of the cold. "It's cold, isn't it? But you want it so bad that you don't care. Get on your knees."

Belle lowered herself one leg at a time. Her wide eyes remained expectant as she stared up at me. I backed away from her, unfastening my belt and then my trousers. By the time I reached the terrace railing, I was stroking myself off with one hand. With the other I beckoned her to come to me. There was no hesitation as she dropped onto her hands and crawled obediently to my feet. She rocked back onto her heels until she was kneeling before me.

I brushed my thumb over her lip, smearing her red lipstick over her mouth, my other hand still on my cock. Pushing the tip of my thumb past her lips, I smiled approvingly as began to suck it. "Do you know why crawled to me, beautiful?"

She nodded but didn't answer, too intent on the finger

she had between her lips. I pulled it away and waited for a response.

"Because I'm yours," she whispered. The dark fringe of lashes fluttered innocently over her large, blue eyes as she answered. She felt the truth of us—understood the primal, irrevocable connection that we had formed. It was an undeniable as our need to breath. It was as captivating as my obsession with her.

"Always," I promised her.

She leaned forward, pressing her mouth to the bulge of my dick. I felt the heat of the kiss through the fabric of my pants and my balls tightened. The way she kept her eyes glued to mine as she worshipped it made my cock throb. It was hard to patient with her offering her body but I didn't want to move. Not while she waited for permission, looking so fucking gorgeous on her knees.

God, I loved this woman. It would be a mistake to think she wasn't the one who was actually in control. She had me, quite literally at the moment, by the balls. I fisted her hair and jerked her head back no longer able to deny myself. Her tongue licked across her lower lip as I pulled my dick out.

"You may," I told her, knowing she waiting for me to instruct her even as I knew what she really wanted.

Belle's tongue lashed out, sweeping along the length of my shaft as she drew her lips to my crown. She swirled the tip languidly before she swallowed me to the root and began to suck.

"That feels so fucking good," I grunted, tightening my

grip on her hair. "I love having my cock in your hot, greedy mouth."

But there were things I loved more and right now they were on display for me. The petite buds of her nipples, the generous curve of her ass. I'd never say not having her on her knees but right now I needed to possess her. I wanted my hands on her body, holding her steady as I took her. I pulled her away by the hair, her lips popping loudly as I broke the suction.

"Up," I commanded, grabbing her under the arm and hauling her to her feet. She liked it rough and I fucking loved to comply. Pushing her forward against the rail, I slid my belt free and wrapped it around her wrists before hooking it over the rail and fastening it.

I left her like that, tied to the railing, naked and trembling in the night air as I rolled up my sleeves. It was quite the sight: the most perfect woman in the world, stripped and bound, against the New York skyline.

"Are you sure you don't want to move to New York, beautiful?" I murmured against her ear. "I don't know were else I can find a view like this."

Her hips wriggled back, searching for contact and I smacked her ass lightly. Tonight was on my terms.

"I'll take that as a no." I fondled the soft mound between her thighs as I spoke until she was whimpering and shaking. "By the time I'm done with you, you might reconsider."

Then I slid deep inside her and gave her something to think about.

# CHAPTER FIFTEEN

*T*he pain shot through me and I twisted, trying to escape it. I cried out, but no sound issued from my throat. I wanted it to stop. I wanted him to stop, but we were well past that point.

*The cane cracked down against my tender flesh and I collapsed. This time it hurt so badly that my breath hitched. My legs burned with the effort of fighting as the ropes bit into my wrists. Smith circled me and I gazed, pleadingly, up at him. But he either didn't notice or he didn't care. He was someone else— someone I didn't know. Where was the man who loved me? Why had he been replaced by this monster?*

I sat bolt upright in bed, my skin slick with sweat. Smith fumbled for the light on the nightstand as I gasped for air.

"What's wrong?" he asked, reaching to soothe me.

I scrambled away, glaring at him. His look said it all. I'd been replaced by a wild creature, my only thought to protect myself.

"It was a dream," he said in a low voice. "A nightmare."

A dream. None of it was real, even though I could swear I felt the sting of where I'd been struck. I wrapped my arms around my chest, hugging my body as I began to rock.

"Beautiful, you had a nightmare," he repeated. This time the truth sank through the fog of sleep clouding my consciousness.

We sat in silence for a few minutes as I gradually came back to the here and now.

"Do you want to tell me?" He spoke gently, and I collapsed at the kindness in his voice. He was still here. He was still Smith. My Smith.

"You...you were beating me," I choked out. "Beating me with a cane."

His lips pressed into a thin line, a vein twitching at the side of his jaw. We both knew what had prompted the dream. It was a subject we had avoided speaking of, but there was no possibility that we could ever fully ignore it. I understood that now. This time when he reached for me, I didn't attempt to escape. Instead I let him pull me against his body. He murmured soothing praise in my ear as he stroked my back. Even then I couldn't let it go.

"Why?" I pushed the question past dry lips. "Why did you do that? Why did you choose her?"

"Because I wanted you to walk away and never look back." His confession was harsh only due to the truth it contained.

I knew that was the reason he'd put me through that scene. But regardless of his intentions, I couldn't dismiss the pain it had caused me to see him striking Georgia in Velvet. Or the betrayal that clung to the memory.

"Why her?" I repeated.

"Because she was willing and because I knew it would hurt you."

I jerked away from him, not bothering to hide the horror I felt.

"Do you still want a submissive?" I demanded. "Someone you can beat? Will you ever be happy with me if I can't give you that? If I won't?"

"I don't want that," he said in a firm tone that left no room for questioning. "I didn't want to put you through that to begin with, and it's certainly not the life I want. Or the life I've chosen. I chose you, beautiful."

"That night you chose her." I spit the accusation at him. "You still like it, don't you? Dominating a helpless woman?"

"No! I don't. That's my past. It's not my future."

"If it's what you needed," I continued, ignoring his answer, "take me there. Tie me up. Whip me. Choose me."

"I already chose you, and I don't need to do those things to you. I want our relationship to be out of pleasure. I want to make you come and make you laugh. I want you to be happy." But the flatness of his response suggested he understood that it was far more complicated than that.

"You asked me to go there. You hurt me and then you came back for me!"

"My hand was forced. You know what I'm trying to accomplish."

"No! I don't!" I exploded. All he'd given me were partial explanations, enough to soothe but not enough to appease the gnawing uncertainty that came with my self-doubt. I felt ashamed for offering my body to abuse at the same time that my desperation grew to manic levels. "Take me there."

"Absolutely not."

His denial stung, and I shook my head. "Not there. You came to New York for a reason. There's a club here surely. Tell me I'm wrong."

He hesitated and I knew immediately that I'd trapped him.

"Where?" I pressed. I stumbled out of bed and began pulling items from the closet. "What do you wear to a BDSM club? Or do I go naked?"

"Come to bed."

But I wasn't giving in this time.

"Take me there. Show me." My voice softened. I couldn't be kept from this part of his life—this element of his past—any longer. "I want all of you. I won't settle for less."

Smith's expression was unreadable as he appraised me. Finally, he spoke. "Wear a dress. Nothing expensive."

"Panties?" I began to tremble as I pulled a simple black shift from a hanger.

"Yes. I'm not putting you on display." He held up a hand when I opened my mouth to protest. "I'll show you why I came to New York. I'll take you to who I went to see, but it ends there. If you fight me on this, I'll put you a flight in the morning."

"You can't dictate my life, Price."

He flinched at my use of his surname, but I was well

past caring. It was time to face our demons and try to survive them. I couldn't live with the possibility that we couldn't. I had to prove to myself otherwise.

FROM THE STREET there was nothing special about the building the cab driver delivered us to. It was past midnight, and there wasn't a soul in sight. The cabbie looked nervously at the spot. "You sure this is the place?"

"Yeah, we're good." Smith tossed a tip in his direction, which effectively silenced his concerns.

Smith didn't reach for my hand as we walked to the door. Unlike Velvet, it opened immediately and the sound of smooth, dreamy music floated toward us. I stepped in behind him and stopped. This wasn't a club, it was some type of late-night theatre. On the stage, a group of scantily-clad dancers performed a sensual number. Two men pushed and pulled, tugging at the woman in between them. She collapsed in one's arms only to have him toss her in the air. The other man caught her, even as her hair grazed the hard wooden floor beneath them.

There were only a handful of people in the audience. No doubt the show was drawing to a close. Turning on my heel, I shot Smith a withering glare, but he looked past me.

"Mistress," he said in a greeting, and I spun around to face an elegant woman dressed in a sweeping, floor-length gown that glistened ruby in the dim, atmospheric light. She was in her mid-forties, her hair cascading gracefully over a bare shoulder.

"You've joined us, and I see you've brought your friend." Her thinly plucked eyebrow curved into a question mark.

"Belle, meet—"

"Samantha," she interjected. "My clients call me Alice, but you're not a client."

It was an explanation of sorts, but I found myself struggling to process what I was experiencing. So this was the woman who Smith had come to see. Judging from the Scottish accent that coated her words, she was someone from his past.

"Welcome to The Looking Glass. It's a pet project." She motioned for us to follow her to the bar. Catching the bartender's eye, she held up three fingers. A moment later, three petite glasses sat before us.

"Absinthe." She lifted one and handed it to me. "It makes the impossible probable."

I swallowed it in one gulp, nearly gagging on its unapologetically licorice flavor.

"She wanted to meet you," he explained, not bothering to take the drink she offered him.

Samantha studied me for a moment with sharp eyes. "I think she came for more than that."

"I came for answers," I said. If no one was going to start talking, I was going to start asking. "Like who the hell you are and why he had to come so far to talk to you?"

"She is a fiery one." Samantha spoke to him as if I wasn't there.

"You have no idea," I warned her.

"You came for answers, but you also came for release,"

she guessed. "From the secrets that are burdening you and the fear that accompanies them."

It was like talking to a goddamn sphinx. If I'd hoped she'd be more forthcoming than my mysterious boyfriend, I supposed I would be disappointed. But nothing surprised me anymore, not when it came to the complicated, thorny relationship I had with Smith.

"Samantha is Hammond's wife."

I'd been wrong. He could still shock me.

"I left him years ago," she said in elaboration. "Smith keeps me apprised of what's going on at home."

"And what did he tell you?" I asked. "Probably more than he told me."

"That a shift in the wind is coming."

More riddles.

"He came to warn me," she continued, waving a hand dismissively as though it was nothing out of the ordinary. "And you came for Wonderland."

"Does this bitch come with a decoder ring?" I snapped, but she only laughed.

"I can see why you aren't taking her as a submissive."

Damn right, he wasn't. I was too busy seething to actually say it out loud.

"You'll take her there and show her. It's the only way to soothe her." Her instructions were clear, and it left little doubt in my mind that Hammond's wife had been as deeply entrenched in London's seamy, sexual underbelly as her husband.

"We'll take a look." His meaning was clear.

But that didn't mean I was going to abide by his wishes.

"You know the way," she told him. Then she leaned closer and whispered in my ear, "Fall down the rabbit hole and open your mind."

My skin crawled from the heat of her breath, but as soon as she said it, she vanished back into the theatre.

"Show me," I commanded. Tonight I was calling the shots, and he was going to have to deal with it. Smith motioned toward a corridor and I strode forward. There was no place for fear here, but my blood still pounded erratically in my veins. I'd asked to come here, and now I would face the thing that scared me the most.

The fear that I couldn't be what he needed.

A door painted in gem tones waited at the end of the hall, and Smith opened it for me. There were more people inside than had been in the audience. Apparently, Samantha had the same penchant for covering her sins as her husband. A few heads turned in our direction, but no one spoke as we passed through the richly decorated lounge. On the far side of the room, a large mirror reflected back the scene before me. A naked couple sat on the couch, and at their feet a woman bound in red rope held the end of a leash in her teeth. After my experience at Velvet, I didn't find this shocking, but it made me queasy. This was the world Smith had once inhabited. It was the world he might still want to be part of, and I wasn't certain I could exist there with him.

Smith bypassed the seating area and went to another door. He paused, as if steeling himself, and opened it. I followed him inside, surprised to find it empty. I startled as a lock clicked into place behind us. I turned my attention back to the only furniture in the room: a strange X that loomed in front of a large window. Peering through the glass, I realized I was looking at the lounge. The mirror I had seen had been a trick. I waved at the people on the sofa, but they stared past me, unseeing.

"They can't see us," Smith said as he removed his jacket. "If we're going to do this, it will be on my terms."

I opened my mouth to protest, but he silenced me with a raised hand.

"I'm not sharing you. I'm not putting you on display," he informed me in a gruff voice. "And I'm not torturing you, but I will show you what I want to do to you."

His words shivered through me and I nodded.

"Take your clothes off."

I rushed to peel the dress over my head. It took several attempts given that my hands were now shaking as badly as the rest of me.

"I'm not going to hurt you," he reassured me. "And as soon as you ask, this stops. Say the word red and it's all over."

I could do that. I could do this. I trusted him.

Didn't I?

Smith took my hand and guided me toward the cross. "Put your arms up."

I placed my arms against the wooden planks.

"I'm going to fasten you to this," he explained. "And then I'm going to punish you for doubting me."

I gulped against the lump that formed immediately in my throat.

Smith buckled a leather restraint over each wrist. Then

he bent down. I struggled to see him, but then I felt another leather strap fastening over my ankle. I was spread before him, naked and bound. I'd asked him to do this, and now I needed to trust that I could live with whatever came next. He stood next to me and slowly unbuttoned his shirt before stripping it off. The sight of him, bare from the waist up, made my sex throb. But this wasn't about pleasure. That's not why I was here.

I was here to be punished.

I wished I could say that the thought scared me more than it excited me, but it didn't. I hung my head in humiliation. This was how badly I wanted him—how much I needed to be part of his world.

"You're stunning," he said. "Your fear makes you more beautiful, and your trust makes you irresistible. I'm so fucking hard right now. I want to fuck you until you beg forgiveness, but that's not what you want is it?"

I tried to nod but I couldn't. Smith's hand caught the back of my neck. "Answer me."

"No."

"What do you want?"

"To be punished," I answered in a small voice.

"Good girl." Smith released me and moved across the room, out of my line of sight. When he returned, I heard the slight slap of something against his palm. A moment later, cool leather brushed along my backside. "Breathe, beautiful."

I forced myself to even as panic swelled in my chest. Then he struck. I flinched but only as a reflex. The tails of the whip barely smacked along my skin. They spread like teasing tendrils over my ass. I felt my flesh warm, but it didn't hurt. Instead the pulse growing between my legs ratcheted up.

"You're already getting wet," he commented. "I can see it. This isn't going to hurt, but you're going to wish it would. Because then you wouldn't have to feel the ache of your cunt with each strike."

I moaned as he lashed me again. The heat radiating through my rear was pleasant, but it wasn't the pleasure I craved. I squirmed against my restraints, my thighs trying to press together for relief.

Smith clicked his tongue. "Only I can grant you release. That's what you want, isn't it?"

I choked out a yes.

"Then ask me to whip you again. This time I won't stop."

"Please, Sir." The request fell from my lips as naturally as a breath.

He complied, swinging the whip in fast, successive motions that stole every thought from my mind. All that existed was the want building in my core, and each time he struck, I willed the tails of the whip to smack against the swelling need at my center. But he knew what he was doing. He would deny me pleasure until he determined I deserved it. My teeth bit against the soft flesh of my bottom lip as I struggled to keep my pleasure in check. He'd pushed me to the edge, and I had to cling to it, knowing he would be displeased if I allowed myself to lose control. But it grew harder as he continued, until the pleas began to spill from my mouth. Wanton. Urgent.

The whip flapped to the floor, and I heard the merciful click as his belt unbuckled. Smith placed a palm over my sex lightly. If I could move, I would have pressed into it and shattered at the contact.

"You're dripping." There was lusty approval in his voice now. He reached up and quickly unfastened each hand. I gripped the wooden cross for support as he undid my ankles and helped me down. "Against the window. You're going to look out at those people you fear while I fuck you, and then you're going to know that this—that what happens here—is between us and only us. It always will be."

He guided me to the glass, and I flattened against it as he wrenched my hips back. The head of his cock nuzzled against my sensitive seam, and I braced myself, knowing I wouldn't be able to control myself when he finally breached my entrance.

"You're going to scream when you come," he instructed in a husky voice. "And you're going to thank me for fucking you—for making you mine."

He paused, the tip of his penis positioned against me, and then he plunged inside. I cracked open, pleasure flooding through me as my cries poured out. Through the window, nothing changed. No one moved. No one looked up at me. I didn't exist to them. I only existed here in the presence of the man who had claimed me as his own.

"That's right. This is what you need. I know that, beautiful." He continued to thrust tirelessly as I quaked around him. And as my spasms calmed, I cried in gratitude.

"Thank you. Thank you. Thank you." I said it because it was the only thought I was capable of. He'd given me what

I needed. He'd centered me even as he stretched me thin and taut. This was what I needed. He was what I needed, and I would never stop marveling at that.

When his pace finally slowed, he lingered inside me. Brushing a strand of hair from my mouth, his lips moved against my ear. "This is what I want—to give you everything you need. Everything you deserve. Nothing else matters."

He gathered me in his arms and held me for a long time, whispering how much he loved me. And I believed him. The realization settled deep inside me, taking root in my bones, as unshakable as the love I felt for him.

## CHAPTER SIXTEEN

The bed jolted underneath me, and I opened one eye to Belle's smiling face. Hoisting my body up, I lounged drowsily against the headboard. She was already dressed for the day in a soft cashmere sweater that made her eyes look nearly gray in the morning light. If she was feeling any lingering doubt about last night's activities, it didn't show. I cupped her chin for a moment and studied her.

"Morning, beautiful," I yawned. The only better way to wake up was when she was still in bed naked with me, but opening my eyes to her smile was a very close second.

"We're going on an adventure," she announced as she crossed her legs under her, revealing a pair of jeans and suede boots. Apparently I'd slept through a shower and who knew what else.

I bit back a laugh at her infectious enthusiasm. "I thought we went on an adventure last night."

"*Not* that kind of adventure," she clarified, raising her

eyebrows before winking at me. "We've spent enough time inside this week."

I didn't miss the suggestive way she said inside.

Inside her? Inside our hotel room? Inside a dungeon? As far as I was concerned, inside was geographical perfection. But it would be unfair to prevent her from spending any time in the city, especially since she'd never been here before. I stretched my arms and reached for her, but she wiggled out of my grasp. "You have me at a disadvantage. I'm not even dressed."

"Uh-uh." She clicked her tongue against the roof of her mouth as she shook her head in refusal. "We leave soon and I haven't seen anything. You're going to have to spend a few hours keeping your hands to yourself, Price."

"Really?" I called her bluff. I lifted the bed sheet and peaked underneath. "Don't be offended, mate. She still likes you."

She swatted my hand away, and I dropped the sheet, taking advantage of the opportunity to catch her. Pulling her into my arms, I shifted so she could feel my erection pressing against her ass.

"I haven't seen anything touristy," she said, nuzzling against my neck. "Take me out, and you can be as handsy as you want tonight."

I had her exactly where I wanted her, and she was negotiating. After spending yesterday with her at whip's length, all I wanted was to spend the day in bed making certain she received hours of pleasure. "If my girl wants to go out, I suppose I need to put this away and get dressed."

"I do want to go out." Her teeth nipped at her lower lip

as she struggled with her own battle of want versus need. "But it would be a shame to waste this."

Her hand slipped under the sheet and found my shaft. That was the kind of conservation effort I could get behind. I flipped her on her back and climbed on top of her before she could change her mind. I'd been wrong—this was the perfect way to start the day.

NEARLY BARE TREE limbs tangled together over us as we made our way into Central Park, their leaves crunching under our feet as we walked hand-in-hand through the green space. Winter was drawing closer, and the chill of the air nipped at our exposed faces. We'd both bundled up for the outing. Belle had managed to find her sweater after our morning lovemaking, but she'd settled for a skirt and tights after we realized her pants were missing in action.

They were under the bed, but I wasn't above playing dumb if it meant I got to spend the day looking at her shapely thighs.

"There's a zoo here somewhere," she said to me, "and a pond and oh!"

She stopped in her tracks to stare at a man painted white from head to toe. He stood motionless, a small box at his feet. Digging into my pocket, I dropped a few dollars into it and the man began to move, blinking and shifting as if confused to find himself coming to life. Belle watched in rapt attention, delight drawing her lips into a radiant smile. After a few minutes, the performance artist settled into a new position, crouching low with his chin resting on his hands.

"I hope he finds a new audience soon," I said we continued along the pavement.

"He will." Belle beamed as her grip on my hand tightened.

There was a magic in the air that seemed to hover all around us. It felt palpable, as if we could catch it if we were patient enough. Maybe it was the peacefulness that seemed to exist here despite the city teeming with life that lay outside its boundaries. Or perhaps it was simply the company I found myself in.

We happened upon the pond by accident and paused there to watch two boys raise sailboats across it. Belle clapped and cheered next to me before she traipsed over to the cart selling the boats and bought two for us.

"Care for some friendly competition?" she asked, bending to place her boat onto the water.

I moved behind her to block the view of her ass. Gripping her hips, I squeezed. "I don't like to lose."

"Neither do I," she warned, her eyes flashing mischievously as she released her boat.

"Cheater!"

"It's not my fault you're so easily distracted." She shook her behind as I rushed to get my own boat on the pond. In the end, she trounced me so soundly that I knew I couldn't have won even without her head start. That wasn't going to stop me from giving her shit about it for the rest of the day.

"You are shameless," I told her as we walked to the

other side to grab the boats. We passed them to a family sitting nearby.

"I can't help winning." She shot me a haughty look.

"Shameless. Competitive," I muttered under my breath. "You're such a Price already."

Belle inhaled sharply at my words, but before I could judge her reaction, she tugged away from me and pointed to the arched entrance of the zoo. She had reacted though. Just as she'd reacted the other night on the terrace as if my suggestions both frightened and thrilled her. They had the same effect on me if I was being honest, but for vastly different reasons.

I paid the admission, and we spent the next few hours wandering through the compact animal sanctuary, enjoying each other's reactions as much as the animals. Near the primate exhibit, a chimpanzee tossed an apple to me and motioned for me to eat it. I took a bite and tossed it back.

"I'm pretty sure that's against zoo rules," Belle said dryly as we continued on before it became a game of catch.

"Animals and I understand each other," I said, wrapping an arm around her waist and drawing her closer. She melted into me, laughing."

"Sometimes I think you belong in a cage," she admitted.

"You're probably onto something, beautiful." I leaned over to whisper, "Later I'll show you how primitive I can be."

Belle shook her head, a giggle bursting from her even as her eyes darted toward a small girl and her mother. Longing flashed across her face, but she smiled widely as the child passed us. It confirmed what I'd suspected. Belle was every bit as interested in starting a family as she was a business. It seemed like a long shot that I had more to do with that than a biological clock, but then again, she hadn't even been interested in dating when we first met.

"What are you thinking about?" she asked, drawing me from my thoughts.

"That I'm hungry," I lied. I wasn't about to share these insights with her, not when she wasn't conscious of them herself. Instead we found a cart selling hot dogs and ordered two. Settling onto a park bench, we ate them, discussing the strange ways Americans dressed their food.

"They can't put all of that on one of these." Belle shook her head as I recounted the hot dog I ordered once in Chicago.

I raised a hand. "I swear."

She opened her mouth for further questioning as a ball of color tumbled over at our feet. Belle reacted immediately, helping the small child to his feet as his mother rushed down the path. The boy had begun to cry, and Belle soothed him in a quiet voice as she brushed debris from the knees of his pants.

"Thank you," his mother said in a flustered voice when she finally reached us. She took his hand and led him away. "You've got to stop running away, Gabe!"

Belle sat back down and watched as the pair made their way to the zoo. There was no mistaking the look on her face. Longing. She wanted a family. She wanted a child.

God, I wanted to give it to her. I wanted everything with this kind, beautiful woman who seemed to inherently understand how to live a full life. I wanted her to teach me how to do the same. I never thought it was possible that I could be a good man. With her, it seemed possible. She made me believe I was more than the sum of my past mistakes.

I'd entertained the thought of more before now but only to gauge how she reacted to the idea of commitment. This was different. It was as if I'd spent my whole life waiting for this moment, and now that it was here, everything that came before it seemed to fall away. I hadn't even known it was waiting for me.

"Are you done?" I wiped a bit of mustard from the corner of her mouth.

Belle eyed me curiously. She hadn't missed the husky undertone that colored my voice. I couldn't pretend as if every bit of me wasn't pulsing with this revelation.

She crumpled her napkin and tossed it into the rubbish bin. When she turned back toward me, I captured her mouth, pouring the promises I wanted to make into the kiss. Her soft hand caught the back of my neck and held me there.

I felt it. I knew she did, too.

We didn't have to talk about it. It was as real—as tangible—as the touch of our bodies. It was also as complicated and tangled as our limbs were becoming as we gave into one another fully. We were only a man and a woman, committing to the basic, urgent call of our biology. I wanted to take her right there and then, but I restrained myself.

"Take me to bed," Belle panted when we finally extricated our tongues from one another long enough to speak.

Neither of us spoke as we dashed back toward the Plaza. Overhead a sudden rumble announced rain moments before the first drops splattered on our cheeks. The deluge was as quick and unexpected as the revelation I'd just experienced. By the time we reached the hotel, we were both so drenched that no one thought anything as we ran toward the lift. It was the perfect alibi.

I couldn't wait for twenty flights. My fingers slipped under the band of Belle's sweater, and I peeled the soaked garment over her head. Wrenching the straps of her bra over her shoulders, I freed her breasts, my mouth closing over her tender nipple as we rocketed up the lift. Her hands splayed against the mirrored glass as I bit and sucked. Reaching under her skirt, I tore at her tights, ripping the seam that covered her pussy just as the lift doors slid open.

There could have been an entire cadre of Japanese businessmen standing there and we wouldn't have noticed. Scooping her into my arms, I carried her toward the suite, unable to keep my mouth off her. Off her lips. Off her skin. She was perfection incarnate—a goddess and a temptress rolled into one. At the same time, she was so much more than that. I could spend my whole life studying the dictionary and never discover all the terms to describe how wild and sensual and fucking brilliant she was.

"I need to be inside of you," I groaned as we slammed against the door. Belle fumbled to undo my pants as I let us inside. We nearly fell, but I caught her against the door.

Shoving her panties to the side, I pushed into her slick cunt. It would take nothing to push me over the edge. I wanted to fill her. I wanted to watch her face as I emptied my cock inside her. But Belle's head fell back as she began to moan.

"S-s-so good," she crooned before crying out in pleasure. "Fuck me, Smith. I want to feel it."

Oh, she was going to feel it. She'd still be feeling it tomorrow, and if I had my say, she'd be feeling it next week.

More dirty words fell from her lips before I crushed our mouths together. She didn't need to ask. I was never going to stop. I was never going to give her up. When she finally tightened around me, I braced her against the wall and hammered us both to a shattering conclusion. But as Belle slumped against me, I didn't withdraw from her. Instead, I cupped her ass, urging her legs around me. Carrying her up the stairs, I laid her in our bed and slowly undressed us both.

Despite my powerful climax, my erection hadn't flagged. She made no protest as I crept over and slid inside her. I could only comprehend this. Her nails digging into my back—scratching across my skin. The brush of her soft breasts against my chest. The slow circle of her hips against the thrusts of my groin.

"You're mine," I growled, pushing onto the palms of my hands so that I could rock deeper into her channel.

I dared to look into her eyes, dared to hope that I would find the same fervent wonder I felt there. Instead I saw fear. I shifted my weight and lifted a hand to her cheek. I wanted to wipe it away—erase the anxiety and doubt that tainted our relationship. But I knew it wasn't as simple as that. All I could do was offer her reassurance that she was wanted.

That she was loved.

Because my God, I loved this woman, and if I had to spend every day proving it to her, I would.

"Forever." I pushed the word out between breaths. "Mine forever."

And longer.

I didn't want her body or her heart. I wanted her soul. I wanted everything down to her last breath.

A tear glinted from the corner of her eye and I kissed it away. She smiled shyly and arched into me, offering me her lips. I took them—captured her kisses, shared her breath— as I took all of her and made her my own.

# CHAPTER SEVENTEEN

*T*he next few days passed in a blur as we tried to jam as much into the remainder of our time here. Sex and museums and shows and sex and shopping and sex. We'd given in to the fantasy of what our lives could be like—and it felt good. Wicked and selfish and fucking amazing. Our impending return to London meant sharing Smith with others, most of whom I neither liked nor trusted. It also meant working out how to mesh our lives together. For the most part, we'd avoided speaking of what would happen when we reached Heathrow. We'd be together. We'd agreed on that. The rest we'd have to sort out.

But when our final night in the city arrived, a heavy pressure built in my chest. It clawed through my breast, searching for an escape, which I was pretty certain would come in the form of hysterical crying or hyperventilating or looking up immigration requirements. Here it had been easy to ignore the trouble waiting for us in London. Smith seemed equally anxious. He spent the morning on his mobile, pacing the length of the terrace as he made calls.

It wasn't how I wanted to spend our last hours here, but I knew he was worried. He'd tried to protect me from his associates before. Now he was planning to take my hand and walk with me into the lion's den. At noon, I peeked outside and found him, sitting quietly.

"Is everything arranged?" I asked as I dropped onto his lap.

Smith's arms coiled around me, and he nodded even as his eyes remained distant. "Mostly. There are a few last minute issues."

"There always are." But my response didn't soothe him. Smith wasn't here with me—not really. His thoughts—his concerns—were elsewhere. As much as I wanted to draw his attention back to me, I understood what was going on. Since I'd discovered the nature of his involvement with his employer, I'd been concerned for his safety. How much worse was that feeling for him?

"I'm sorry, beautiful. I have to take care of a few things." He planted a kiss on my forehead. "How about dinner? I'll arrange reservations for seven."

"Okay," I said slowly, "but that gives me a lot of time to go shopping."

This earned me a grin, but it faded too quickly. "Take my card. I added you to my accounts."

"I have my own money," I protested.

"Belle"—Smith grabbed my chin and forced me to meet his gaze—"we have money. Get used to it."

I didn't argue with him further. Instead I decided if he

was going to insist that I make a dent in his bank account then I would go shopping for him. Not that the man needed clothes. That didn't stop me from purchasing a variety of new ties, which was admittedly a bit selfish on my part considering how I hoped he'd use them. As I passed the men's jewelry counter at Saks, I stopped in my tracks.

"Can I see those?" I asked, jabbing at the glass.

"Lovely taste," the associate remarked as she removed the gold feather cufflinks from the display and passed one to me. "Unique but elegant."

But my thoughts were caught in the past, recalling the gentle, exciting introduction I'd had to Smith's sexuality at the touch of a feather. I swallowed, wishing I was with him now. "I'll take them."

I tried not to feel guilty as I passed her his credit card. As much as I wanted to buy them from my own money, I knew that wouldn't merely deplete my account but it would probably carve a giant sinkhole in it as well. I resisted the urge to chicken out as she handed me the card slip, and a few minutes later, I'd tucked the carefully wrapped package into my purse.

Although I probably had more time to kill, it seemed like a good idea to stop now. But when I checked my mobile, it was only four in the afternoon.

Research. I wouldn't buy anything, I thought as I headed to women's fashion. But it was part of my job to be on top of the market. It occurred to me that I probably should have spent more time in New York working on that. But an hour of research was better than nothing. I was already going home without an interview. Neither Lola nor Katherine had been in touch with more news.

The spring lines were beginning to filter onto the racks, but many of the pieces I happened upon were the same. Since there was no rush to launch at breakneck speed, we needed to be purchasing the lines as they came out. I pulled out my mobile and shot off a text to Lola. It was the middle of the night in London, but I didn't want to forget to strategize that with her. It was already five, so if I headed back now, I'd have time to get ready before the car arrived. After a day denying myself, squeezing in a bubble bath seemed like a good compromise.

I had nearly reached the escalator when a mannequin caught my eye. There was no fighting it. I had to see the price tag. I had to touch the fabric. The sleeves were barely capped, and although the neckline didn't so much as reveal the collarbone, there was a classic sexiness that was impossible to deny. It was something more than a little black dress. Perhaps owing to the full skirt that draped gracefully to the floor in the back but that swept up in a slight angle to fall mid-calf.

"You should buy it," a familiar voice advised me as I studied the gown.

I pivoted to find Katherine Harper behind me. "Peer pressure, huh?"

"That's not just a dress, that's a statement." She paused as we admired it.

"I'm not sure I have an occasion for something like this. It might be a bit much to wear to dinner with my boyfriend."

"The occasion is wearing it," Kat said with a laugh, tucking a scarlet strand behind her ear. "Wear that and something magical will happen."

"You should work here." She already had me sold.

"I might apply after the week I had." She chewed on her lip nervously. "I'm so sorry again about what happened."

"Don't worry about it," I stopped her. "If I let every bitch who spoke cruelly to me stop me, I would never have gotten here in the first place."

"Sounds like you have some perspective on this."

"You should meet my mother."

"Look I'm working on Abigail. I don't know what crawled up her ass"—Kat's hand flew to her mouth. "Sorry! I just mean she's been a little hostile lately. In a month she'll be pitching me a female entrepreneur story. I'll keep you up to date."

"Thank you." It was easier to say that than to tell her not to bother. Abigail Summers had burned a bridge with me. Life was way too short to deal with thundercunts.

Katherine continued to chat with me while I had the sales associate ring up the dress. I was almost to the hotel when Smith texted me.

SMITH: Ran out on some business. Car will pick you up at seven.

So much for the miraculous qualities of the gown. If I was lucky, he would be there on time. I chose not to be upset though. We were both here on business. If I made myself up and sat alone at the dining table, there was always wine.

Every once in a while a woman puts on a piece of

clothing or a pair of shoes and *magic*. I'd seen that magic on Clara's face when she stepped into her wedding gown. I'd felt it when I put on my first pair of Louboutins. It sounded ridiculous, and it wasn't something I could explain exactly. Except that some clothing was transformative. As I zipped up the black dress, I felt that magic settle over me.

I didn't bother to look in the mirror as I slipped on a pair of simple black heels. It didn't matter how I looked. Not in this dress. It was how I felt. I was a princess on the way to the ball. I was Audrey Hepburn catching every man's attention in the room. I was Belle Stuart, and I was fabulous. As I entered the lobby, the heads swiveling to watch my progress told me I was right. A bellman ran to open the door as I approached and I smiled at him.

"You look lovely this evening," he complimented me as I swept past him. "Do you need a car?"

"I have one picking me up at seven." I glanced around, looking for a private sedan.

"Ah, Miss Stuart?" he guessed.

I nodded and he pointed to a long, sleek limousine idling at the curb. The driver jumped out and ran to open the door. I accepted his help getting in, wishing Smith was here with me. Leave it to him to spoil me even when he wasn't around to enjoy it. I didn't ask where we were going. Instead I looked out the window. We cut through Central Park, and my mind drifted to the day we had spent there. Something had shifted that afternoon. Smith had shown me a vulnerability that was uncharacteristic. Making love had been raw and passionate, and most notably, not kinky. And yet it was the sexiest night of my life. There'd been no distance between us—no exchange of power. And although I enjoyed it when he got rough or ordered me around in bed, that night had been about connection.

Like the weekend before he fired me. Like the last weekend we'd spent openly as a couple before we pretended to break up—and before we'd actually broken up. I pressed my hand to my stomach as it lurched. Tonight was our last night together in New York. We were supposed to go home to London as a couple, but Smith had made it clear that he would always choose my safety over our happiness.

He was going to try to end things between us. And I wasn't going to let him.

Not this time.

My safety wouldn't matter if I couldn't stay away from him, and nothing was going to separate us again.

*Except an ocean,* a little voice interjected. Smith had expressed his interest in staying in New York. It wasn't something I wanted to do. But he'd spent the last few days saying goodbye to me. The more I recalled the time we'd spent together, the love we made, the more obvious it became. He wanted to show me he loved me—prove it— before he left me again.

I swallowed against the tears building in my throat. Why would he fix me if he was only going to break me again?

*Because he does love you,* the voice said. It was a rational reason. Perhaps if he could prove his love then it would be easier to know he was making a decision to protect me. But love wasn't rational or patient or easily dismissed. Love consumed and changed. Love took two people and joined their hearts. Distance, death—nothing could separate them. And if life ripped those hearts apart, there was no way to ever heal, too many pieces were missing.

I refused to let the tears fall, just as I refused to let him walk away. If there was danger we would face it together.

There were no other options.

I repeated this silently, willing the words to take shape so I could cling to them for strength, as the limousine slowed to a stop in front of a spectacular glass cube. A large blue sphere glowed inside the nearly dark building.

"Excuse me," I called to the driver. "Do we have the right address?"

But he was already out of the car and opening my door. "The Rose Space Center. That's where I was directed. I'll wait here for you."

I was going to have a chat with Smith about his strange desire to reroute me mid-trip. I somehow doubted there was much food inside. I took the driver's hand and stepped out of the car. "It doesn't look open."

As if on cue, a security guard appeared, stepping toward the entrance. "Miss."

I was so flustered that I realized I left my clutch when I reached him. For a second I considered going back for it, but curiosity won out. The interior was dimly lit, giving shape to a variety of exhibits that were closed for the evening. The guard entered behind me, and I turned to him with hands spread.

"Follow those," he advised, tipping his head to the ground.

I followed his gaze to discover two rows of candles. Their flames flickering into a path. I walked slowly, slightly concerned that my skirt might knock one over. I was so focused that I stopped in surprise when I reached a doorway. It was so dark that I couldn't see inside. I gripped the frame and stepped cautiously through. As my heel touched the floor, a million glittering lights lit up the space. I stared up in wonder as the night sky appeared before me. A star soared into blackness in the distance. I was so mesmerized that I didn't hear Smith approach until he took both of my hands. Opening my mouth, I found myself speechless.

"I found the stars for you," he said in a low voice that was rich with husky emotion.

"It's beautiful." It was the most I could manage to say. He'd stolen all my words just as he'd stolen my heart.

"You're beautiful." He held out my arms and studied me. Here we were under the most dazzling display of stars I'd ever seen, and Smith couldn't look away from me. "Every day I wondered what I did to deserve finding you. Every day I question why I get to keep you."

"Smith," I began but he shook his head and I fell silent.

"We're going back to London tomorrow."

This was it. I swayed shakily on my feet, and he caught me around the waist. "Don't," I pleaded. "Don't leave me again. I won't let you."

"I'm not leaving you," he promised softly. The faint starlight shadowed half of his face, etching the rest in brutal, magnificent lines. "Never again."

His words freed the tears I'd kept confined during my ride here. He brushed them from my cheeks as they began to fall.

"Hold out your palm," he instructed me in a gentle voice.

I turned my trembling hand over and waited.

"I'm not getting on one knee. I'm not asking. This isn't an engagement ring." Even in the darkness, the band he placed in my palm glinted with fire, the diamonds catching the light of the stars overhead.

"I don't understand," I admitted as I stared at the ring.

"It's our future. It's our life. That's a wedding band, Belle. It's in your hands now—along with my heart and everything else I have to give you." He closed my fingers over the band. "You're what I want. You're the only thing I've ever wanted. I've been waiting for you my whole life. Now my life is yours."

I barely processed it as he kissed me, and when he backed away, he didn't press me to speak.

"It's up to you. There's the door. There's the ring."

"Smith, I..." But I didn't know how my own sentence ended.

"Our lives are complicated. This isn't."

I opened my hand and picked up the ring. It felt complicated—and heavy—and a million other emotions that didn't have words.

But he was right, this was up to me.

# CHAPTER EIGHTEEN

"*L*'ll have a gin and tonic."

Belle raised her eyebrow as if she disapproved of my choice of beverage. "Tea."

The flight attendant moved on, scribbling down our order.

"A little early to start drinking," Belle commented when the attendant was out of earshot.

"Time does not exist in a straight line, especially on an airplane." I glared at the console dividing our seats. "I've never been jealous of the economy cabin before."

"I think you can make it seven hours without touching me." But she moved her hand to rest where I could hold it.

"At least I don't have to completely keep my hands off you." I studied her as she relaxed back into her seat. "You should get some sleep."

"That's not what you said last night," she said with a wink.

"Last night I was trying to convince you to see things my way." I glanced down to her naked ring finger. "I see you aren't wearing it."

"Smith." She paused, her pale eyes searching my face. "I just need a little time before..."

"The ring doesn't matter." I lifted her hand and kissed the spot where it should rest. "It's an object. Nothing more."

She belonged to me, and I belonged to her. I needed to focus on that.

Belle closed her eyes, our hands still clasped. "I don't think I'm ready."

My chest tightened at her words, and I pressed my lips together. It wasn't what I wanted to hear, but she had every right to express her opinion. "I'll have to prove you wrong."

"I meant I don't think I'm ready to go back to London," she clarified, not bothering to smother the exasperation she felt. "Although I do love when you prove me wrong."

"It doesn't sound like it, beautiful," I teased. "Don't hold it against me. Providing evidence to the contrary is my job."

"You aren't my lawyer," she reminded me, propping open one eyelid.

"Consider me a witness for the defense."

"Are you defending yourself?" she asked.

"I've gotten quite good at it over the years."

The light banter had proved my case. I needed to move her attention away from the trouble brewing at home. After staying up all night, showing her exactly what I had to offer as part of my proposition, she needed rest. "Sleep," I repeated.

"Why does that sound like a threat?" She yawned as she spoke, frowning when she realized I was right.

"Because it is a threat," I told her. "Once I have you home, you won't be sleeping much. Last night was only a preview of what's to come. There won't be a divider between us forever."

"I might have to take a separate bedroom. Maybe you were onto something at your old house," she said, referencing the private quarters I'd given her. She hadn't once slept in them.

"Our house. Our bed." I liked the sound of it, and from the way she grinned sleepily, she did as well, even if she was going to be a little shit about it. No ring, but she had agreed to move in. Not that it had even been up for negotiation. I needed to be assured of her safety at all times. I assumed we had two days—a week at the most—before news of our domestic arrangement reached Hammond. That would give me enough time to hire a private security detail and a driver. That hadn't been a part of the discussion either, and I knew when I finally revealed the expectations, she wasn't going to be happy.

She'd have to learn to live with it—and me.

"You're so demanding." Another yawn. "Caveman."

"Later I'll throw you over my shoulder and show you how primitive I can be. But for now, sleep."

Her eyelids drifted down, and a few minutes later, her breathing took on a steady rhythm. The flight attendant returned, and I sent back Belle's cup after accepting my own. Sipping the cocktail, I memorized the peaceful, dreamy expression she wore, etching the curve of her cheekbones and the dent of her lip. I stored the image deep inside me where I kept all my memories of her. It was a place that couldn't be touched—that couldn't be stolen from me. No matter what happened, I would have those moments until I drew my last breath.

Abandoning my drink, I absentmindedly rubbed my own bare finger. I'd once thought wearing a wedding band was worse than being collared. I'd watched acquaintances and colleagues accept the shackles and then proceed to spend the years complaining about their restraints. Most of the people I knew who married wound up divorced. I had no doubt that Margot and I had been on the way there ourselves when she died. I'd already spoken to a lawyer, the same one who'd drawn up our prenuptial agreement.

I'd made a mistake marrying my first wife. I'd been young and blinded by her dazzling smile. But I'd protected myself.

There would be no need for that with Belle, which was why I'd walked into Tiffany and purchased the diamond band that she'd relegated to her carry-on. I'd made my decision. Now I just had to convince her that I hadn't lost my mind. My thoughts returned to the night before. She was lucky there was a divider or I'd start working on my case immediately.

Suddenly London felt even farther away. I groaned and spread a blanket over my lap. Sleep felt like a very good idea. She needed rest, and I needed to escape the erection that was bound to last more than four hours. Belle sighed in her sleep, her lips turning up at the corners, as if she'd heard my thoughts in her dream.

"Sweet dreams, beautiful," I muttered as I adjusted my cock and closed my eyes, reminding myself that I could, in fact, keep my hands off her for seven hours.

Even if I didn't want to.

CHAPTER NINETEEN

eathrow was a zoo when we finally made our
way through customs and headed to get our
luggage. I took each step slowly, dreading what lay before
me. I hadn't mentioned to Smith that I'd failed to tell my
friends that I didn't need a ride from the airport. Instead I
held his hand, leaching whatever strength I could in preparation for the inevitable confrontation waiting for me.

I spotted Edward's curly hair before we'd reached the
bottom of the escalator. He was dressed casually in a pair
of jeans and a long t-shirt. No doubt in an attempt to blend
into the crowd. Not that he could if he wanted. More than
a few people were whispering excitedly as they passed him
by, but he didn't seem to notice. My stomach lurched as his
eyes scanned the crowd, searching for me, and I silently
cursed Lola for not being the one to come inside to
retrieve me. Edward's gaze landed on me as we stepped off,
and his welcoming smile vanished immediately when he
saw I wasn't alone. It was too late to disappear into the

crowd. I'd been spotted, and from the looks of it, there was no way I was escaping an explanation for the sudden reappearance of my ex-lover.

Where was a firing squad when you needed it? I'd much rather be facing one of those than the disappointment plastered across Edward's face.

Edward glared at me as we made our way toward him at the baggage claim. He caught me in a hug as soon as we reached him, muttering, "Most people bring home a t-shirt as a souvenir."

"Watch it," I warned him. I knew there was no way to avoid this fight. I'd known it when I purposefully chose not to cancel his plans to pick me up.

Edward straightened up, puffing his chest a little as he stuck out his hand. Smith accepted, shaking it. The gesture was courteous on both parts, but it was far from friendly. The two had a long way to go.

"If you two are done beating your chests, can we get the luggage?" I darted away, leaving them to continue their show of masculinity.

Smith followed me, grabbing my hand and spinning me toward him. I didn't have time to process anything but the firmness of his lips on mine as he captured my mouth in a deep, possessive kiss. A self-respecting girl would have pushed him away, but I melted into him instead. When he pulled back, he shook his head. I'd hear about this later.

Two fights in my future, and I'd only just hit solid ground.

"I suppose you'll be riding with him," Smith said, glancing over his shoulder. Edward glowered back.

"Yes." This wasn't up for debate, but he didn't fight me on it.

Smith retrieved our bags, but he didn't pass mine along. "I'll take this to the house. See you there tonight."

I winced as I nodded. There was no way Edward was going to miss that.

He grudgingly handed me off to my best friend with another kiss goodbye and made his way toward the car park.

Edward said nothing as we left. When we reached the pavement, Lola waved to us from the driver's seat of her car. She frowned, tipping up her sunglasses as I climbed in beside her.

"Did they lose your bags?" she asked.

"Nope. Bags are safe," Edward answered for me. "Her mind is another story."

"Should we go then?" Lola sounded as confused as I felt.

"Yes," I said with a sigh.

She popped her glasses down and hit her turn signal as she made her way into the airport traffic. Lola didn't require further explanation, but I knew I wasn't getting out of this that easily.

I pinched the bridge of my nose and braced myself, but Edward remained silent. I'd completely sidelined him. I knew that, but I didn't deserve the silent treatment. This was hardly the first time anyone in our close-knit group of friends had made up with an ex. I'd expected reproof, but it didn't make it any easier to bear, especially with Edward sitting like a giant, seething lump of disapproval behind me.

"Are you going to yell at me or what?" I finally snapped when I couldn't stand it any longer.

"For what?" he asked. "I have no bloody clue what just happened."

"Is this about the bags?" Lola's eyes darted to me and I shook my head.

"This is about Belle getting off the plane with Smith Price," Edward informed her.

"What?" Lola exclaimed, squealing in excitement.

"No! We aren't happy about this," Edward interjected, flopping against the back seat.

"We aren't?" she asked. Looking over at me, she repeated herself, "We aren't?"

"He isn't," I explained. "I'm...confused."

"Did you go mad? Price treated you like shit. He hurt you! So badly that you wouldn't even talk about it. How the hell did you even run into him? Aren't there millions of people in New York?"

Lola bit her lip as if she was holding something back. Edward couldn't see the gesture from his seat, but I caught it. She shot me a guilty look over the rim of her glasses.

"I told him she was going," she admitted in a quiet voice.

"Do you mind pulling over?" Edward asked. "I don't think either of you are sane enough to operate a moving vehicle."

"Oh, sod off. She's an adult."

"That's questionable," he muttered.

"You told him I was going to New York?" I asked her.

"It was more like I bragged about it," she said, tapping

the steering wheel nervously. "I caught him slinking around outside the office."

"You what?" This was news to me. "You might have mentioned that."

"Well, I didn't know why he was there, so I told him you were busy getting ready to head to New York for an important interview. Look, I thought I was doing you a favor. No man likes to hear that their ex is moving on."

She had done me a favor, even if Edward was glaring murderously at her.

"Thank you," I said sincerely. "We spent some time together and talked."

"And then you shagged each other, and he managed to convince you to come crawling back."

That stung. Edward had no clue how complicated things were between us. But now, more than ever, I needed his support.

"I'm in love with him," I announced. "And if you don't like it, you can suck a big one."

It came out more immature than it had sounded in my head. Next to me, Lola began to shake before she dissolved into giggles.

"Noted," she said between laughs.

"I just don't want to see you get hurt." Edward appeared unmoved by my proclamation.

I swiveled in my seat and met his gaze. "I don't need your approval, but I'd like it anyway. Your opinion means a lot to me. I know Smith can be a little hard to get a handle on."

"Impossible, you mean." He exhaled and then smiled. "I

want you to be happy. I just hope he doesn't cock things up. Promise me that you'll take things slowly."

Now didn't seem like a good time to mention the diamond wedding band burning a hole in my purse. I hadn't been sure what to expect when my friends found out that Smith was back in my life. Thankfully they had no clue how precarious our situation truly was. I'd keep that— and Smith's unorthodox proposal—to myself for the time being.

"I will," I lied.

"So when he said he'd see you at home..." Edward trailed off, leaving me scrambling for an answer.

In the end, I went with the truth. I'd have to keep enough from him in the coming months as it was. "I'm moving in with him."

"We have very different ideas of what taking it slowly means," he said flatly.

"I never moved in with Philip. I'm not making the same mistake with Smith." It was a pitiful excuse, and judging from Edward's tight-lipped reaction, he thought so, too.

"I heard from several designers," Lola said, switching the subject. I shot her a grateful smile.

"Which ones?"

She rattled off a list, but my thoughts were elsewhere. Tomorrow I needed to focus on Bless, but right now I was still reeling from all the changes I'd brought home with me. Smith had seen this coming when he asked me to uproot my life. That's why he'd left the decision, quite literally, in my hands. I was the one who had to live with the consequences. The only comfort was that I'd be doing it with him by my side.

JET LAG WAS the perfect excuse to escape the uncomfortable tension that permeated the car, and as soon as I was in my flat, I dropped my bags. Drooping against the door, I tried to fight how deflated I already felt. Edward's disapproval agitated me. I didn't like being on the outs with a friend, especially over a man.

Especially since that man was going nowhere.

But there was nothing for it, and Smith expected me across town. After sleeping on the plane, I was wide-awake and somehow still exhausted. Tomorrow I had to get my butt in gear. Tonight I had to sort through the events of the last twenty-four hours.

My gaze traveled through the flat's open floor plan. This flat, and another just like it, had been my home for the last year and a half. But the sense of comfort I usually found when returning through its doors was absent, replaced by restlessness. I didn't belong here anymore, but did I belong at Smith's? Both options felt like little more than shelter at this point.

"I thought I heard you." My aunt swept into the room in a pair of silk pajamas. "You look tired."

"I am and I'm not," I told her as she reached for a bottle of wine. "None for me."

"I'll drink a glass in your honor then," she said dryly. "Dare I ask about the trip?"

"I wouldn't know where to start." I slid onto a chair, propping my elbows up at the table.

"How was the interview?" she asked as she poured herself a drink and joined me.

I snorted. How was it possible that the least interesting aspect of my business trip was the actual business? "It was a no go. The editor proved to be a first-rate bitch."

"At least you have experience dealing with that type."

"Speaking of Mum, has she called you?" I already knew the answer.

"Daily." Jane's lips pursed in distaste.

"I'm sorry. I'll deal with her tomorrow." Add that to the list of chores I was dreading. I still hadn't bothered to look at the paperwork she'd sent over regarding the estate. I'd meant to call my brother and have him review the documents. Instead I'd wound up across the Atlantic. It seemed I was turning avoiding my mother into an art.

"It doesn't matter. What else do I have to do? Frederick locked himself in the studio to finish his latest opus."

Despite the chaos I found myself in, I smiled. Listening to Jane discuss her conquests was the best distraction in the world, but even her wild stories couldn't completely deter me from thinking about my own romantic entanglements.

"You've been married. Why?" I blurted the question out of nowhere.

Jane sat her glass slowly on the table. "I take it there's a reason for this question."

My cheeks burned but I managed to nod.

"I have, and I haven't." She shook her head and sighed.

"I've had husbands, Belle, but I've never really been married. That sounds crazy, doesn't it?"

"Yes," I admitted, laughing with her.

"Men have asked me to marry them, and I've complied. Some died. Some left. But I never truly felt married to any of them."

"I guess that explains why some days you're an old maid and others you're a divorcée." Jane's twisted idea of lovers had always amused me, even though it also confused the hell out of me.

"Some days I'm more one than the other." She tapped her glass. "I'm guessing you want to know why."

I did want to know, because right now I needed to understand—understand why some people got married and others didn't. And why some marriages lasted a lifetime and others failed. I was grasping for answers I wasn't certain existed, but I was more than willing to listen to anyone that would talk about it.

"I loved a man once. If that sounds like the start of a sad story, it is."

"What happened to him?" I asked her in a quiet voice.

"Life. Pride. Fear. It's much easier to pretend to make a commitment you don't really intend on keeping than it is to face the prospect of giving everything you are to one person. That takes trust."

"And you didn't trust him?"

"I didn't trust myself," she clarified, running a hand over her platinum hair. "And by the time I did, it was too late. He married someone else."

"Do you still miss him?"

"Every day. I regret it. Lovers distract me, but no one has ever filled the void his absence left in my life. Maybe that's why I said yes whenever a man asked me to marry him. I was scared that I might look back on that relationship with the same regret."

"So if you could, would you change it?"

"I'm an old, wealthy woman who's seen more of the world than most. The politically correct thing to say would be no. But yes, if I could go back, I would change things." She shrugged, her eyes growing distant. "Perhaps I would have regretted that course of action. I'll never know and I guess that's what eats at me."

She settled against her chair, her gaze zeroing in on me. "Now tell me why you asked."

"Because I'm afraid." I swallowed hard on my confession. It was difficult to admit that I was scared of what I wanted most in the world—precisely *because* I wanted it.

"Then take my advice, love. Do what scares you. It's what keeps you alive. It's far better to live with the regret of a relationship that doesn't work out than to live with the pain of loss." Reaching across the table, she took my hand in hers. "I'm guessing you have a lot more to tell me about New York."

"Yes," I whispered. But I wasn't ready to share yet. Not until I'd come to grips with my own decision.

"When you want to tell me, I'll listen." She didn't pressure me for more information.

Tears smarted in my eyes, and I gripped her hand fiercely. "Thank you."

"If I have to live my mistakes, at least you can learn

from them." She squeezed my hand before releasing it. "Now do you want a glass of wine?"

"No, there's someone I need to see."

"I thought there might be," she said wisely. "Don't be afraid to trust your heart, Belle. It's your compass, let it guide you."

I nodded, even as my world spun around me. How was I supposed to follow my heart's direction when I couldn't be still enough to know where it pointed? The only thing I knew was that right now it was pointing me to a house in Holland Park. I couldn't see further than that, but journeys began with a single step. I was ready to take the first one.

CHAPTER TWENTY

*I*t was the first time we'd met in person, but I took no stock in this changing the nature of our arrangement. The only thing that had brought me to him was my own desire to escape my tangled past, and a sense of obligation to the people Hammond had destroyed. I couldn't be certain which was more important to me. Not anymore.

He didn't offer me a drink as I took the seat opposite him. I didn't even warrant a handshake. There had never been a time for pleasantries in our relationship and today would prove no exception.

"My expectations were made clear." It was an icy welcome, but the one I had expected after I'd received his message this morning.

Undoubtedly, news of my sudden appearance at the airport with Belle had already filtered up to him. That was the consequence of allowing her friends to see us together. Considering she arrived at my house—our house, I corrected myself—with packed bags the night before, it was better to face the repercussions now.

I gripped the arms of my chair, but restraint when it came to this subject wasn't my strong suit. I bristled at the thought of explaining my choices to him. "I'm the one who has to live with my decisions."

"But you aren't the only one who will live with the consequences," Alexander growled, transforming from cold and impassive to ferocious instantly. It was a trait well suited to a king, but not one that I particularly admired. His shoulders squared in challenge. We were matched in size. But that was where our similarities ended. We each viewed ourselves as in control of the board and the other as a mere pawn.

"I agreed to participate in this witch hunt," I reminded him in a low voice. If he was going to choose dominance, I would show him that control was a key element of that path. A fact that he'd never understood in our long and sordid history. I'd watched him rise and fall and then ascend the throne. I respected that journey, but I also saw the truth behind his own willful determination. "I didn't seek her out. She was sent to me."

"And when you realized why, you continued to use her," he accused me, his blue eyes flashing. "You were instructed to discontinue your relationship with Belle Stuart."

I leaned forward, placing my palms on his desk. "I'm Scottish. We've never been very good at taking orders from a king."

"You should have considered that before you came to me seeking absolution."

"I came to you because you sought out the information I had, and in doing so, I broke every tenant of my profession." Now I was seething. If I didn't manage to calm myself, I'd regret more than my words.

Alexander glowered at me. His disgust with my actions was as evident as his concern for Belle's safety. It was the only reason I hadn't shown him just how little I cared for his overbearing directives. I loosened the knot of my tie and forced myself to sit back. The more distance I kept between the two of us, the better.

For his safety.

"I can't assign added security to her if you two continue to see each other openly." He said it as a warning, but the reminder was unnecessary.

"I'm aware of that. I assure you" I clenched my fists, cracking my knuckles to release the tension building within me. "Her safety will remain my concern."

"Has it ever concerned you?" Alexander folded his arms behind his head and swiveled in his chair to face his window.

I hoped he found comfort in the views of his garden. "You've lived a life of privilege. You've never wanted for protection. I don't expect you to understand that, outside the walls of a palace, the world doesn't bow to other men's whims."

"You think my desire to ensure her safety is a whim?" He didn't bother to turn back to face me. In his mind, I was no more important than any other servant. "You're so much colder than I thought, and I've always considered you heartless."

I was out of my seat before the last word left his lips. My hands slammed down on the table, but Alexander didn't move. "I think that you have no idea what you're doing or this would be over by now. I gave you everything you needed to prosecute him for his crimes months ago. You've had him in check, but you've made no move."

"We aren't playing chess, Smith. And I'd remind you that I am the King. I'm the one who must decide if a threat is removable."

"Then what's stopping you? Hammond is expendable. The threat dies with him. The only people he's ever groomed to replace him have betrayed him."

Alexander turned then, his face a stony mask as he regarded me hovering over him. "You'll excuse me for not entirely trusting a man capable of such deception."

"I had nothing to do with the attack." This wasn't the first time that I'd stated this fact, and I had a feeling it wouldn't be the last. Not while he clung to his paranoia. It was clear no amount of evidence would convince him that Hammond was the only person he needed to worry about. "You know he's the head of the monster. Cut him off and the rest will die."

"I don't want to cut him off." He spoke through gritted teeth. "I want him to suffer. I want him to know fear."

"Then I'm not the one risking anyone's life." I stepped back and shook my head, my contempt now matching his. "You have the power to bring this to an end, and yet you refuse to stop it."

"He murdered my father."

"Let's not pretend that your obsession stems from a

need for filial retribution. We're beyond that. This is insanity."

I'd had enough—enough of the cat and mouse game. Alexander had made me a target. Now he was effectively making Belle one as well.

"You're right," he said, surprising me. "This has very little to do with my father. In the event that my personal role in Hammond's fate is ever revealed that's how the story will be spun. Who could blame a man for seeking his father's murderer? Who could judge a man that assassinated an assassin? It's a matter of national security."

"But it's more than that to you," I pressed.

"It is much more personal than that," Alexander hissed. "You provided me with the evidence that Hammond aided Daniel on the day of my wedding. I was never the target that day. Nor was my father. For reasons that are still unclear to me, Hammond wanted him to kill my wife. I suppose that part of me does want retribution for my father's assassination, since he was the one who prevented her murder."

"That is something I can understand." And I did. The thought of Belle becoming another victim was impossible to bear. But it didn't remove his culpability for not bringing the man to justice.

"That surprises me." He folded his hands in his lap and regarded me with a calculated gaze, as though he might be able to see through me and my intentions.

"I don't care if you doubt my empathy for your situation, but I won't continue to sit back and allow you to do nothing." Or was that what he was playing at? If he waited, one of us would be forced to take action ourselves. Why should a king do his own dirty work?

"I told you I wanted him to suffer. Not because of my father or what he did to me, but because I know beyond a shadow of a doubt that he's made three attempts on Clara's life. He fueled Daniel's perverse delusions. Not once but twice. And when that didn't accomplish his ends, he sent someone on a suicide mission to run her off the road. I want to know why, and then I want to flay him alive."

"And that's worth continuing to risk her life? You're as heartless as I am." I spoke flatly, understanding now that no amount of reason would breach the mad spite the man clung to.

His fingers steepled, pressing together so tightly that the tips turned white. "Says the man risking the life of a woman he claims to care for."

"I love Belle. I don't take the danger she's in lightly. It would behoove you to show the same concern for Clara."

"Clara is my wife," he shot back. "And as such she is my concern."

"And Belle is my wife," I exploded, "so she is also very much my concern. My only concern."

Alexander fell silent, studying me as if to ascertain the validity of my claim.

"We were married in New York," I continued in a cold voice. "I will not live without her. Not for king and not for country."

"That complicates matters."

It was the understatement of the century. "Tell me something I don't know."

"You will protect her." He released a deep breath as he rubbed his temple. "And I can do very little to help you in that regard. Hammond will find out, of course."

"I assumed as much, but I also assumed we were much closer to ending this."

"Now we'll have to be."

The atmosphere in the room shifted as two opposing forces melded into something unfamiliar. No longer were we two men grappling for authority against one another. For the first time since we'd begun this quest, I felt allied to the man sitting before me.

I dropped back into the chair facing him. "I never intended to force your hand."

"Perhaps you should have. I underestimated your commitment to her."

"In your position, miscalculation can be a dangerous weakness." He needed to be reminded that his duty wasn't to his own petty vengeance, but to the people he claimed to love. I wouldn't apologize for being the one to make him see that. I wouldn't apologize for anything I had to do to ensure my wife was safe.

"We have days then." Alexander reached for his mobile and shot off a text. "You took precautions to contain this information."

"Yes." Belle and I had agreed to keep our marriage secret even from our closest friends. Not that I had anyone to share the joyful news with. Only her. But if it was a hardship for her to deceive those she loved, she hadn't fought me. I suspected she was still processing her decision.

"He'll still find out. You should be prepared for that. I told you that I didn't understand why he persists in coming after Clara. My only theory is that he does so in an attempt to get to me." Alexander shook his head, as if it were impossible to understand the man's motivations. "Had I known the first time she was attacked that there was more to what had happened, I would have gone to any lengths to protect her, even if it meant giving her up."

"And yet you didn't," I pointed out.

"When I understood the true nature of the situation, she was already carrying my child."

I stared him down. No man that loved as possessively as him could actually walk away. "And if she hadn't been?"

"I don't waste my time pondering that. She is my life. I chose her."

"Then choose to do what it takes to protect her." This time, I was the one giving the order. His obsession had to end, and swiftly. For all our sakes.

"I will."

It was as solemn a vow as I had made to Belle. It left no room for doubt in my mind.

Standing, I stretched out my hand and Alexander took it, sealing our mutual understanding. Relief washed through me. The life that I dreamed of—for her—was finally within my grasp.

I turned to leave, but as soon as I reached the door, I came face to face with the object of Alexander's mania. Clara stood outside his office, her arms wrapped protectively around her waist. She glanced up at me with searching eyes. But I didn't have the answers she sought. I didn't know this woman, but I knew what she meant to him—what she meant to my wife. So I inclined my head. It wasn't a gesture of deference but one of concern. Alexander had kept this from her. That much was clear from her pale, sickly expression. I wished I could do more or offer her some comfort, but that was his job now. I didn't dare come between her and Alexander, even momentarily.

It was time for each of us to face our fears. Ignorance was no longer an option, nor was inaction. I could only hope she was as strong as the woman I'd fallen in love with, but despite how little I knew of her, I'd watched her grace in the face of public pressure and tragedy. Alexander had been wrong to hide the truth. He would have to deal with the fallout.

We all would.

# CHAPTER TWENTY-ONE

*I* would never get through all of these emails. Apparently every person I'd reached out to in the last month had chosen to respond to me while I was in New York. Lola had failed to mention that we hadn't heard from some designers, we'd heard from nearly all of them. I couldn't help wishing that I'd spent more time working and less time in bed with Smith during our brief overseas holiday.

"You are a strong, capable woman," I said out loud, simply because I needed to hear it, even if I didn't quite believe it. Maybe it would be easier to sell myself on the idea once I was on top of things again.

By noon I was considering throwing my laptop across the room when my phone vibrated.

CLARA: I'm stopping by. Okay?

I responded that it was more than okay and waited with my eyes glued to the door lest I reconsider my decision not to smash my computer against the wall.

Clara arrived with a sagging diaper bag, cradling a pink bundle. I swiped Elizabeth from her arms immediately, cuddling my godbaby closely. Elizabeth curled her legs up and nuzzled into my shoulder. She was so tiny and delicate still. I could hold her for hours and never grow tired. Instinctively I began to rock her.

"Careful or she'll spit up on your shirt," Clara advised, hovering nearby.

"That's okay," I cooed, kissing her velvety forehead. "Auntie Belle doesn't mind."

Clara held out a burp cloth, her eyebrow arching as I took it and maneuvered it under Elizabeth's head.

"What?" I asked as I continued to sway with the baby.

"You have baby fever," she accused.

My mouth fell open. Of all the ridiculous accusations, that had to be the worst. Business fever? Yes. An unrelenting passion for shoes? Obviously. Completely punch-drunk in love? That was undeniable. "Would you prefer I didn't want to hold her?"

"No." Clara shook her head and held out her arms. "But I'll take her back now."

My eyes narrowed and I turned away from her outstretched hands. "You get her all the time, and I've been away for the last week."

"I think that proves my point." Clara's tone couldn't be drier if she shoved a bag of cotton balls in her mouth. "And speaking of your trip, tell me about it."

I turned back to her, studying her suspiciously. She wanted to hear about more than my trip to Central Park or my interview. On the surface, her blue eyes were as glassy as the surface of the ocean on a windless day, but underneath that facade of calm, the waters churned. I knew her too well not to see that.

"There's not much to tell." I hated lying to her. I hated the way the deceit clawed through me, scratching at my stomach and squeezing my heart. I'd done it before, keeping Alexander's letters hidden to protect her from more heartbreak. But I didn't have a selfless excuse now. Even if I had my reasons.

And judging from the pain flashing across her pale features, she already knew much more than she was supposed to.

I took a deep breath and made a judgment call. "I'm back with Smith."

Clara nodded, but I didn't miss the slide of her throat. She knew more than that.

Christ, how much did she know and why?

"This morning, I overheard a rather odd argument. I was walking by Alexander's office, and he had a visitor."

I felt the blood drain from my face, and I took a step back until I felt my desk chair bump the back of my thigh. I definitely needed to be sitting down for this one, especially if I was going to be holding a baby.

"My husband was talking to a man I've never actually met," she continued, her voice breaking as she spoke. "And they were fighting. About what happened the day of our wedding. Stop me if you already know all of this."

"Clara, I don't...I didn't..." I couldn't process what she was telling me. "You have to believe me that I didn't know anything about this."

"Nothing?" she demanded, swiping furiously at the moisture pooling in her eyes. "Because that man knows you, and from the sound of it, he knows you intimately."

"Not nothing," I admitted. I wouldn't feign ignorance. She had never met Smith, but she knew enough to guess it was him in Alexander's study. A numbness spread through me as her words sunk in. Smith and Alexander. It was unfathomable.

Smith had been involved with this since long before we met, which meant the two had known each other longer that I'd known him. And suddenly all the half truths he'd told me began to click together, forming a realization I wished I could ignore. I had been sent to Smith—to get to Alexander and Clara. And the times he'd pushed me away hadn't only been to protect me, it had been to protect them as well.

Elizabeth began to whimper in my arms. I rubbed circles on her back, wishing for a moment that I were the one being held. I longed to be innocent and blameless—only capable of need—because now I couldn't differentiate between needing and wanting.

"Start being honest with me and quickly." Clara's sternness took me aback.

I'd never seen her like this. She was scared, that was something I was familiar with, but she was also fearless. Whatever information I had to give her, she could handle it. My best friend hadn't always been that way.

"Smith. I don't know where to begin." I hesitated, searching her face for some sign that she didn't hate me, but coming up empty-handed. "He's been working to bring a man named Hammond to justice."

"Hammond?" she repeated in breathless horror. "The jeweler?"

"He's a little more than that," I told her flatly. I really wished Lola had gotten around to setting up the office bar that we had discussed.

This time it was Clara's turn to sink shakily into a seat. "I don't understand."

"Honestly, neither do I." I could only hope she saw how earnestly I meant that.

"What else?"

I had a feeling that she had heard a lot more outside that office door. It hurt that our relationship had been reduced to a test. I didn't know what she had already found out, which meant the only way I could hope to pass her examination was to tell her everything I did know.

"I didn't know he was working with Alexander." It seemed important to get that fact on the table right away. "I had absolutely no clue that they even knew each other."

"Wait, that's not entirely true," I stopped myself. "An acquaintance of Smith's said she knew you both. It didn't occur to me that it might be important until now."

"Who?" Clara asked in a hollow voice.

"Georgia Kincaid."

Her face blanched. She didn't have to say a word. She knew Georgia as well as I did, which wasn't to say all that well. But we both knew the most vital information regarding her. I wanted to ask her how she knew, but considering the way she clutched her chair as if she was barely staying upright, I thought better of it.

"I guess you've met her." The joke did nothing to lighten the mood.

"Alexander hired her to keep an eye on me after Daniel got into our house. Obviously she did a fantastic job keeping tabs on him since he managed to get through security on our wedding day."

"I can't say that I like her."

"But none of that explains why any of this is happening." Clara chewed on her fingernails as she spoke.

Standing, I brought Elizabeth back to Clara to occupy her hands. She took her daughter and held her close, pressing her face against the baby's petite head. When she looked back up, tears streaked down her face.

"It's going to be okay," I whispered, wishing I believed it.

"Is it? Because none of this feels okay. Alexander would barely talk to me when I confronted him." A sob punctuated her words. "And now I find out that you're keeping things from me as well."

"I didn't want to." I knelt by her side, placing my hand on her knee. "I didn't know you were involved. If I had..."

"What?" she demanded. "You would have told me? Excuse me if I don't buy that."

I sat back on my heels, stung by her accusation. "I didn't want to worry you when I found out that Smith was involved with these people."

"And what about the fact that you married him?" she shot back. "Were you worried about telling me that, too?"

My mouth fell open. So that was what she'd been holding back. I searched for an excuse, a reason that would account for how terrible the revelation made me feel, but I came up empty-handed. "We haven't told anyone," I said meekly.

"My invitation must have been lost in the mail." She looked away from me, her thick hair cascading over her shoulder like a dark curtain falling between us.

"Believe me, you didn't miss much. The butler at our hotel married us in our suite." A vice grip squeezed my heart at the memory that I'd kept secret since that night. Sharing it put me in an impossible position. God, I wanted to tell her the details and giggle and marvel that I was married. But the circumstances surrounding our union made that impossible. Perhaps that was why the ring was still tucked into a box in my purse.

"I'm not anyone. My best friend. My husband. You've all been lying to me, and I don't know how I'm supposed to feel about that."

"We were trying to protect you." That much was true. That much I understood. Clara had endured more fear and pain in the last year than I could even imagine. I hadn't wanted to add more weight to her shoulders.

"By lying to me. The people I love don't trust me enough to support them."

"Would you have supported me?" I blurted out. "Because I'm not even sure that I made the right call."

"Then why did you do it? Why did you marry him if you knew the kind of man he was?"

Anger burst through me, setting my blood on fire.

"Because I'm the only one who knows what kind of man he truly is."

"Edward told me he hurt you," Clara said in a flat voice. In her arms, Elizabeth stirred and I watched as Clara lowered her to nurse.

This was what was supposed to be preoccupying her now: caring for her child. The joy she should have felt had been stripped from her, and I didn't know how to give it back to her.

"Smith tried to break things off." She deserved an explanation, and if anyone could understand the complicated nature of falling in love with a powerful man, she could. "Now I know why."

"So you knew the danger and you chose him anyway?" Clara sucked in a breath. "Belle, I won't lie. I'm angry with you, but I'm also terrified for you."

"Do you think I'm not scared? Because I am. But I'm more scared of losing him—and losing you. Right now all I want to do is escort you back home and lock you away."

"You sound like Alexander." Her nostrils flared and I wondered just how much of a tongue-lashing he had received this morning. "I had to sneak out just to come here."

"You didn't," I exclaimed. Popping onto my feet, I grabbed my mobile from my desk.

"Don't you dare text him."

I paused, torn between the duty I felt to each of them. It was foolish to let her run around without protection, but I hated the idea of betraying what fragile trust might still exist between us.

"I love you too much to let you put yourself in more danger, and you love her too much"—I pointed at Elizabeth, who was still suckling contentedly—"to risk her."

Clara's eyes narrowed, and I knew then what it was to choose the safety of someone you loved over their happiness.

"I'm sorry." But I could tell my apology meant very little to her.

"Use mine," she said before I could continue the message. "Call Norris. He'll come for me, and then you won't have to deal with Alexander."

I raised an eyebrow. "I can deal with Alexander."

"I can't," she said softly. "I love him. I love you. But right now I want to be alone. Norris will understand that."

I decided not to argue with her. Alexander's personal bodyguard had always been capable of maintaining a much cooler head when it came to Clara, and I knew he wouldn't allow anyone to harm her. Digging her mobile out of her diaper bag, I dialed his number and explained the situation.

Neither of us spoke as we waited for him to arrive, and when he finally came to retrieve her, Clara didn't spare a glance in my direction. No goodbye. No hug.

I'd told Smith I had a life to return to in London. Now it seemed I didn't.

## CHAPTER TWENTY-TWO

*I* stayed at the studio, not ready to face Smith but not able to work. As evening approached, I realized I'd done nothing but stare at my computer's screensaver for the last few hours. Grudgingly I forced myself to stand and gather my things. My eyes landed on a pale pink blanket strung over the back of my chair. Clara had left it.

Whatever stability my hours of numbness had given me dissolved. They were my family—Elizabeth and Clara and Edward. I'd lost sight of that, and now I'd done what might prove to be irreparable damage to my relationships with them. I picked up the blanket and held it to my chest, closing my eyes and wishing to be set free. For all of us to be free.

But wishes were for fairy tales, and I had no hope that the universe had any interest in sending me a miracle.

I folded Elizabeth's blanket and stuck it in my purse before I locked up and walked to my parked car at the end of the street. I'd return the blanket tomorrow, and I'd apologize to Clara—and then somehow we'd find a way to move forward. Because I wasn't about to lose my best friend.

The Mercedes's lights blinked as I hit the unlock button. At least at this time of night there would be no traffic. After Clara's visit, I wanted answers only Smith could give me. I'd known he was deeply entrenched in a plot to bring Hammond down, but the fact that he was working with Alexander still stunned me. As had Clara's confrontation regarding my spontaneous marriage.

I'd agreed to keep that a secret, and it shredded me to know that she'd found out before I could tell her. Before she'd even had a chance to meet him.

Clearly I was losing my mind. And that left me feeling uprooted. Smith was my anchor, but was he dragging me down? It stung to admit I might have made a mistake. Mostly because I hadn't even had time to come to grips with the sudden change in my life.

Opening the door, I moved to drop my bag on the passenger seat when I realized I wasn't alone.

Hands grabbed me from behind before I could process this fact. I kicked out, trying to free myself. But the hold on me tightened. The man shoved me against the side of the car, knocking the wind from my lungs.

I couldn't breathe, which meant I couldn't fight.

Fingers closed over my hair, jerking my head back.

"Such a fancy car for such a pretty lady."

My stomach roiled, and I choked against the bile that rose in my throat as I struggled to find my own voice.

*Scream*, a voice deep within me commanded. I opened

my mouth, and his hand clamped over it, catching the cry for help before it could take flight.

"No, no, beautiful," he chastised me. "None of that now. Why don't we go for a ride?"

Beautiful. Hearing that from this strange voice, so intent on humiliating me and probably much worse, spurred something inside me. That wasn't his word. He had no right to call me that. Just as his hands had no bloody right to my body. Whatever fear locked me into place shifted, and I threw my elbow back. I knew with absolute certainty that I had to stay out of that car. The jab caught him in the ribs, and he lost his grip on me, giving me just enough time to twist away.

But not enough time to run.

He caught the back of my shirt and I tripped, crashing to the pavement in a heap, my ankles twisting underneath me. Pain shot through my leg, but I forced it away. Scrabbling forward, my nails raked against the concrete as I attempted to regain my footing.

The man hauled me back, and I heard the nauseating rip of fabric as my blouse tore at the shoulder. I wriggled, hoping that I could shrug it off. Right now it was the only thing holding me captive. But my attacker was too quick. A heavy weight pinned me to the ground, and my chest constricted as I fought to breathe under the massive burden.

"You aren't going anywhere," the cold voice informed me. His hands snaked underneath me, feeling along my body. My stomach. My breasts.

Another wrench, and I felt the cool night air on my skin

as my shirt fell open, exposing my bare back. His knee pressed into my tailbone as his hands continued to wander down.

This wasn't happening.

I wouldn't let it. The scream I'd sought broke past my lips, rupturing the quiet night.

"Shut up, bitch," he snarled.

But I wasn't about to do that. I continued to howl. Someone would hear. Someone had to.

The sickening sound of my zipper stole my cries, and I writhed, my hands splayed out and searching for salvation from the rough cement. My fingers brushed something cold and metallic, and I grabbed my keys, hitting every button in the process and setting off the car alarm.

"You shouldn't have done that," the man yelled, tearing them from my hands. But it was too late. The Mercedes wailed for help as he frantically tried to shut off the alarm.

And then silence.

The street was still empty. No one had heard, and now he had my keys. Gathering every ounce of my strength, I bucked against his hold, knocking him off me. I rolled, and before he could jump back on top of me, I swung the heel of my shoe directly into his stomach, narrowly missing his groin.

The miscalculation cost me. Rather than dropping him, the strike only made him more infuriated. His hands closed over my throat. The sharp edge of a key pressed into my skin. My legs continued to kick, but I made no contact.

"You're a stupid little girl." Spit splattered over my face, and my head fell to the side, afraid of being so close to this man's mouth and the hatred spewing from it.

He grabbed my chin and yanked my face back to his, his other hand still clasped tightly around my neck. His fingers spread up, covering my mouth and then he plunged them inside, wrenching my jaw open. I bit down, but I couldn't get the momentum I needed. He laughed as he held me there.

Trembles wracked my body.

"I just wanted your car, you stupid bitch." His knee smashed into my stomach, and I arched up, gasping for air I couldn't find. "Now maybe I'll take something else."

I collapsed under him, panting, as tears pricked my eyes. I stared up at him, my willpower deserting me. I pled silently with the stranger, even as I memorized the crook in his nose and the long scar that ran along his temple.

If I stopped fighting, what would happen? Right now it seemed like my only choice. I made peace with the fact that I wasn't walking away unscathed, but I decided then and there that I would walk away. I remained still, bracing myself for whatever came next.

"That's right," he crooned. "You want it, don't you? You're hot for it. Can't let anyone know that a classy lady like you likes to be fucked, can you? Got to put up a little fight. But I got what you need, baby."

My body spasmed, and I choked on the vomit I could no longer hold back. The man dropped his hold on me, and my head rolled to the side as I coughed up bile.

"Dirty bitch," he screamed. His hand grabbed my hip, his weight shifting as he flipped me onto my stomach and yanked up my skirt. "This is a much better view. I bet you like it everywhere."

A fingertip hooked around the strip of my thong, and I began to shake. Inside I screamed but the sound was trapped. I was frozen in place, completely at the mercy of evil.

And then I heard the sirens. I didn't know if they were coming for me, but they were there and the sound gave me the power to cry out.

"Fuck." The hand disappeared, but he didn't get off of me.

I knew then that we were both calculating the same thing: how much longer?

"You got lucky this time," he hissed, flattening his body against mine so he could hiss in my ear. "But don't worry. I'll find you, baby, and finish you off. I know how bad you need it."

His groin circled my ass as I began to sob.

"I hate when a woman cries." His hand closed over the back of my head, seizing my hair. He pulled back and captured my mouth, his tongue darting between my lips. This time I bit. Hard. Iron flooded over my tongue just as my face smashed against the pavement. Pain seared through my temple, but before I could process what had happened, he'd slammed me down again.

I knew then that I was going to die. Through the agony, Smith's face flashed in my thoughts. I didn't want him to blame himself. I didn't want it to end like this, but as my neck snapped back and concrete rushed to meet me once more, I knew there was no stopping the darkness.

# CHAPTER TWENTY-THREE

*M*y heart pounded as I bypassed the check-in desk at the hospital's emergency entrance, striding instead toward a nurse's station when I reached St. Mary's.

"Belle Stuart," I barked at the nurse sitting behind the counter.

She glared at me and pointed to a chair. "Only immediate family is allowed in to see her. The doctor is with her now."

"I am her family." Impatience seethed through me. I didn't have time for this woman or her petty rules. I needed to find my wife. I needed to see her. If no one was going to tell me where she was, I would find her myself. I slammed open a door marked Authorized Entry Only with a small thank you tacked onto the bottom. Trust the British to be polite in every circumstance. That was one trait I hadn't been born with. I had too much of my mother's blood in me.

"Sir!" the nurse called behind me, but I was already down the corridor, my eyes darting into every open door.

I could feel myself getting closer, but with each step I took that didn't bring me to Belle, the furious panic building inside me swelled. I hated hospitals. I hated the stench of sterile death that permeated their halls. I hated the cold, impersonal interiors created to give you nothing to cling to when you were given the worst news.

This was the only time I'd stepped foot in one since Margot had died. The doctor's platitudes floated to mind as my brain prepared itself to relive that day. Only this time it would be worse.

It occurred to me that I was on the eighth floor, high enough to ensure I wouldn't survive if I could find an open window. My unease grew, and I began to open the closed doors, not bothering to shut them. Angry protests filled the air as I ravaged my way down the hospital wing.

And then she was there. Eyes closed, monitor softly beeping.

A pair of hands closed over my shoulders, hauling me away from her room, but I jerked away.

"Sir, you need to come with us," a security guard advised me, one hand on the baton hooked on his belt. Another stood silently a few feet behind him.

"That's my wife," I informed him through gritted teeth. "I was told immediate family was allowed in."

"They are," he responded calmly, "but we need to check your identification first, and frankly, it's up to the hospital if they want to press charges."

I tugged my suit jacket down, willing myself to regain

my composure. "Call Dr. Roget and tell him Smith Price is visiting a patient. He'll vouch for me."

"We can do that in the lobby." The guard gestured for me to follow him outside, but I didn't budge.

"You can also tell Dr. Roget that I'll be donating a generous sum to the children's wing in gratitude for the care my wife receives. I know they need to hire a new oncologist."

The guard inhaled deeply, and I could tell he was weighing his options. A man who took his job seriously would drag me to the curb. A good man wouldn't be able to ignore the offer I'd just extended.

"Stay with him," he ordered his companion before turning back to me and leveling a finger at my chest. "I hope your story checks out, because I will personally see that the only hospital room you visit is your own."

I didn't bother to respond to his threat. Because I didn't give a damn. My story would check out, and Roget would get his money. It felt kinder than blackmailing him with the details of his relationship with a certain mutual acquaintance. Although I'd bring Georgia into the picture if it became necessary. I grabbed Belle's chart from the end of her bed as I went to her side. It was easier to read the status of her injuries than it was to look at her. Contusion to the right eye. Hairline fracture to her right cheekbone. Ten stitches to the temple.

Inconclusive evidence of sexual assault.

My knees buckled, and I dropped to the ground. I didn't believe in God, but I prayed then as I pressed my head against the mattress. I prayed for forgiveness that I didn't deserve. I prayed for her eyes to open. Not to absolve me—I didn't want her to—but so that I could look into them and find the strength to leave her.

Because if I didn't, I was going to kill her. It wouldn't be my hands that did the deed, but her blood would be on them all the same. I'd been selfish. There was no denying it now, each beat of her heart on the monitor reminding me that she'd almost taken her last breath tonight.

"Mr. Price," a clipped voice greeted me, and I lifted my head to see a young doctor enter the room. She rounded the bed and collected the clipboard. "I'm Dr. Grant. Your wife is going to be fine. We gave her a little sedative to help her sleep. I can see you've already reviewed her condition."

"Has she been conscious yet?"

"She woke up in the ambulance and stayed awake for most of the procedures. She was cognizant enough to ask us to call you."

A few minutes ago, I would have been throwing that in the nurse's face. Now I only cared about one thing.

"The chart says there was inconclusive evidence of..." I trailed away, unable to say the words.

"Most of her clothing was still intact when emergency crews reached her."

"What does that mean?" I choked out, my hands balling into fists.

"Her underwear was still on," Dr. Grant said softly, "but we did find evidence that she had recently had sex. I know this is a very personal question, but when was the last time you engaged in sexual relations with your wife?"

"This morning," I answered immediately, "and twice last night."

Dr. Grant blinked in surprise and glanced down at the chart. I got the feeling she found my answer impressive, but I didn't give a shit. "It's very possible then that the DNA we recovered was yours."

I didn't want to consider that it might not be.

"When will she wake up?" I asked. I had to see her eyes flutter open one more time. I had to tell her that I loved her. Just as I had to believe she would understand why I could no longer put her in this kind of danger.

But there was one more thing I had to know. "Did you catch him?"

"No." She shook her head sadly. "It appears to be a random carjacking gone bad. Her purse was recovered from the scene. I'm sure the police will catch up with him."

I gave her a grim smile. "I'm going to stay with her."

She didn't deny the request, which was smart because it wasn't one.

Random. That was one word that definitely didn't apply to this case. A carjacker didn't attack a woman and leave her purse. This was targeted and purposeful, which meant Hammond had found out about us much sooner than I had hoped.

Forcing myself to stand, I dragged a chair next to her bed and sank down into it as I dialed a number on my mobile. The time for retribution was at hand.

I woke to a hand brushing across my forehead. Lifting my head to discover I'd fallen asleep in the worst possible position, my eyes met hers. Belle's face was swollen, a purple rim circling her eye, and she was still the most breathtaking thing I'd ever seen.

"Hey, beautiful," I murmured as I sat up and took her hand.

"Do I want to ask for a mirror?" She licked her lips as she spoke.

I shook my head. "No need. You look gorgeous."

"Liar," she accused with a faint smile that didn't reach her tired eyes.

"Do you remember what happened?" I asked her, steeling myself for her answer.

"Some asshat tried to steal my car, and I was stubborn about it."

I swallowed and forced myself to ask the question I didn't really want answered. "Did he...did he rape you?"

"No." She winced as she tried to sit up. I sprung to my feet to help her, part of my burden lifting from my shoulders. It didn't make any of this okay, but I couldn't help but be relieved.

"The hospital wasn't sure," I explained.

"He made it pretty clear he was thinking about it." Her eyes darted nervously to meet mine. "Would it have mattered if he had?"

"It would have mattered in how quickly I'm going to end his life." There was no point in pretending otherwise. Hammond was at the heart of this, but whatever goon he'd sent to handle his dirty work would find himself paying the price as well.

"Smith." But the plea in her voice was lost on me.

"Don't worry about that right now," I said in a soothing voice. Leaning down, I brushed my lips gingerly over her forehead.

"It's not your fault," she whispered.

But we both knew that wasn't true.

"Belle, I can't allow this to continue." My words came out in halting fragments, each one more difficult than the last.

Tears welled in her giant blue eyes but they didn't spill over. "Sorry, Price. I made my choice. You're stuck with me."

"Not if it means—"

"I know our wedding was a bit unorthodox," she interrupted me, "but I'm pretty sure we got to the vows and all that stuff about death and parting, sickness and health."

"You can't ask me to ignore this," I said, more harshly than I'd intended.

But she didn't shrink away. Instead she sat up and glared at me. "No, I can't. But you're my husband, so you're going to have to deal with it."

I closed my eyes, trying to bite back the smile tugging up the corners of my mouth. "Are you ever going to listen to me?"

"You like it when I provoke you," she reminded me.

I couldn't deny that was true.

"I couldn't live with myself if something happened to you, beautiful."

"And I wouldn't want to live with myself if I ran away. I guess we'll have to learn to live with each other."

It was reckless to listen to her—reckless to give in to

what my heart wanted. But when the doctor came in a few hours later, I was still there. I had put her in this position, and I couldn't desert her now, not while she was so vulnerable—not while I was still breathing.

I'd claimed her as my own. She was mine to protect, and maybe it was foolish to covet her after tonight's events, but she belonged to me and no one was going to take her away until they dragged me to hell.

# CHAPTER TWENTY-FOUR

$\mathcal{A}$s the Bugatti pulled to the curb outside the Westminster Royal I turned to Smith in surprise. We'd stopped by my flat for a few things, narrowly avoiding Jane who was out on an errand. When we had left, I'd expected to return to one of his houses. Not that I had anything against luxury hotels, but I was beginning to think his paranoia was getting the best of him.

"First, no purse. No identification. No mobile." I sighed deeply. "And now a hotel?"

"It's best to be on the safe side." He didn't meet my eyes as he said this. He'd avoided looking at me since we left the hospital. He'd even turned away while I changed in the bedroom of my flat.

"The police said this was an isolated incident." I repeated their words, wishing I believed it. It was better for Smith if I, at least, pretended I did.

He didn't respond; instead I followed him inside. The penthouse suite was every bit as lavish as one would expect from a five-star hotel. Even though it occupied an entire floor that overlooked the Thames, it reminded me of the suite we'd shared in New York. How was it possible we were only there a few days ago?

"You should get some rest," Smith called as he took my bag to the bedroom. "Or eat something. We can order in."

He was treating me like a patient, which only reminded me of what had happened. It wasn't as if the constant stabbing pain that occupied half of my face wasn't memento enough.

"I slept at the hospital." I paused, my eyes finding the floor. "I can't face another nightmare."

Smith reacted almost instinctively, taking me into his arms. He was careful to turn my body so that he didn't touch any of the swelling. "I'm here now, beautiful. Let's watch a movie."

He didn't want me. Not like this. Any other time, he would have taken me to bed and claimed me. The fact only made me feel worse, but I forced a smile.

Smith arranged the suite's sofa so that I could stretch out next to him. We settled in, his arm draped carefully over me as he flipped through channels. Finally he found an old black and white classic playing late on a BBC channel. But I wasn't interested in the drama on-screen, not while my whole life was in turmoil.

I was in a strange place under the influence of a cocktail of drugs that seemed intent on luring me back to the nightmarish realm of my memories.

"I've never seen this," I announced, wanting his attention on me.

"Seriously? We're going to have to educate you in Humphrey Bogart then." He stared down at me with a look of such pure love that my heart constricted, feeling as if it might explode.

He still loved me, despite what had happened. But another man's hands had been on my body tonight, sullying the bond that I shared with Smith, and no matter how hard I tried to escape that, it clawed at me. I felt raw. Vulnerable. I didn't want to sleep, and I didn't want to be awake. I couldn't face this, and he seemed content to pretend nothing was wrong.

But everything *was* wrong, terribly so. I clamped a hand over my mouth and then scrambled up to the bathroom. I sank down in front of the toilet, positive that I was going to vomit. My stomach heaved, but nothing came out except desperate gasps and dry, choking sounds. Smith rushed in and knelt at my side, gathering my hair.

"Are you sick?"

I shook my head. I wasn't, not physically at least. That this was all in my head made it harder to bear. The heaves of my chest turned to sobs that racked through me.

"I'm sorry." But my tears cracked my voice, making it hard to speak.

"You have nothing to be sorry for." He released my hair and dropped to sit next to me. "Nothing."

"Then why are you so scared to touch me?" I was being hysterical. I knew that, but I couldn't control how I felt any more than I could take back what had happened.

"Do you think that I don't want to?" he asked. "I'm afraid I'll hurt you or…"

"Or?" I prompted. I needed to know how that sentence ended, needed to know that his every thought wasn't caught up in how to extricate himself from the mess we were both in.

"I want nothing more than to make love to you right now," he said in a hushed voice, brushing a finger down my forearm. "Not fuck. Not dominate. I just want to feel myself inside of you, but that's not how this works."

"Why not?" I challenged, growing angry at the idea that we were both denying what we needed.

"Because it's my job to take care of you, and I've already fucked that up enough."

I couldn't stand the anguish pooling in his green eyes.

"I need you to show me I'm still yours. That you still want me."

He stood and my heart splintered along the fissures that had barely healed from the last time he had broken it. Someday there would be no heart left at all, only scar tissue. But tonight, my heart could still feel and the agony Smith inspired was far more acute than any physical pain I'd endured.

But then he bent down and lifted me to my feet before scooping me into his arms. He carried me slowly into the bedroom, whispering the vows he'd said to me only nights before. Laying me carefully across the bed, he stripped off his clothing until he was bare. His cock bobbed as he approached me and hooked his fingers over the waistband of my pants. He drew them off in one fluid motion.

"In the hospital, when I saw you there, and you were breathing, do you know what happened?" he asked as he palmed his dick. "I got hard. I wanted you so badly that I had to hide my erection with a pillow. You know why, beautiful? Because I always want you. Because your very breath is mine, and it hadn't been taken away from me. I needed to stay away from you—needed to not touch you—because I couldn't bear to make you suffer."

"Don't stay away," I cried, my hands struggling to slide off my panties. "I need to know you still want me."

"This time when I say we have to do this on my terms"—he lifted my leg and bent to kiss the softness of my inner thigh—"it's not because I want to dominate you, it's because I won't be able to forgive myself if I cause you pain."

Our relationship had always been about pain commingling with pleasure. It was what had brought us together, and now that intimacy had been robbed from us. More than anything, I wanted to pretend nothing was wrong. I wanted to crawl to the edge of the bed and take his cock into my mouth, but I knew he wouldn't allow it. And his control over this situation was the only remnant of what we had shared only this morning.

"I want to see you," he rasped. He leaned over me, hovering to keep his weight off me. I wanted to pull him down and force him to release the primal masculinity he kept from me now, but I remained still. Smith ran his fingers down the neckline of my camisole, his eyes pinned to my face. "I want to be careful, so I hope you aren't attached to this."

He pinched the fabric in both hands and stretched until the threads gave way. He had no way of knowing that another man had ripped my blouse from me tonight, just as he had no way of knowing that simple act done with the utmost care and concern had erased that memory, replacing it with an image of love. He opened it gently, freeing my breasts to the air and then slowly slid the tattered remnants away.

His fingers danced over my skin, dodging the bruises left behind by the attack, and then he began to kiss me. Smith's mouth moved lower, his lips and tongue flickering across my skin with a light touch that reminded of the tip of a feather. Tonight there would be no playful whips and smacks though, but there would be want. Want that consumed me like a flame blazing into a fire. Want that vanquished any fear I felt.

There was no fear at Smith's hand. No trepidation. He'd taken my body and given me his very soul in return.

"I'm going to make you feel good, beautiful," he whispered, his breath tickling over my abdomen. "I'm going to take all the pain away for as long and as often as I can."

My head fell back against the sheets as he dipped his tongue between my thighs. He licked along my seam with a reverent patience that drew the attention of my nerves until all sensation in my body was centered there. He kissed the plumping flesh of my mound, sucking the whole of it fervently into his mouth. A low moan emanated from his chest, and I bucked against the vibration it sent trembling through my skin.

Oh god, this man. This sinful, cocky, broken, perfect man was going to make me come without ever breaching my folds.

He drew back as soon as my abdomen tensed and hooked his arms under my thighs, yanking my legs over his shoulders. His hands slid down to cup my ass, holding me in the air as he kissed my tortured pussy.

"I'm not through with you yet. I only wanted to make sure I had your undivided attention."

That sounded a lot like a promise. I grabbed the sheets and held on.

"I love burying my face in your ripe cunt, tasting your sweetness on my tongue. I just had to stop and admire how pretty you look with your legs around my neck and your pussy plumped and ready for me. I'm going to take good care of you both. Forever, beautiful."

He kept his eyes on me as he lowered his mouth to fuck me. I watched, white light creeping into the edges of my vision, as his tongue parted my slit. The tip of it flicked across my clit until I was gasping and pleading. But he wasn't ready to let me go yet. He flattened his tongue, stroking the length of my sex languidly. I writhed beneath him, nearly vaulting out of his grip. Digging his fingers into my hips, he rocked me back and forth against his tireless tongue.

"Please, please, please." The word fell from my mouth with each sweep of his tongue over my clit.

He paused just long enough for my want to throb painfully through my core, and then his mouth clamped greedily over my engorged nub.

My back arched off the bed as I ground myself against his mouth. There was nothing but him and the pleasure he poured through me. My anchor. My release.

When he finally lowered me to the bed, I sagged bone-lessly, my legs sliding from his shoulders and my climax still pulsing at my core.

"You got so fucking wet when you came." He groaned as he nudged the head of his cock against my slick entrance. "I'm going to be tasting you for weeks."

I bit my lip shyly, my eyes drooping as I prepared myself for more.

More and never enough. That seemed like a pretty solid foundation to build a future on.

"I can feel your cunt squeezing my tip. Does it want more?"

"Yes, Sir," I panted.

"No, not tonight. Tonight you're my wife—*my partner.*"

"Your equal?" I teased.

"You're always that." Smith licked his lower lip. "I only hope I'm yours."

He was in every way. I wanted to tell him that. I wanted to press my body to his and feel this man who belonged so entirely to me, and I to him. But before I could find the strength to move, he slid inside me, effectively destroying any possibility of me moving. Not when he was piercing me to the core. Not with him rooted fully inside me.

We began a slow, sensual rhythm. Neither of us rushing as we lingered in the sensation of our union. He filled me, and I consumed him until we were one body, melding and morphing into a perfect symphony. Our tempo increased gradually as we rocked together, but then Smith stopped and withdrew.

I missed him immediately, longing for the completeness only he could grant me.

He moved farther up the bed, propping his back against the headboard. "I need to hold you."

I rolled to my stomach and crawled to his lap.

"Slowly," he urged as I lowered myself, one hand guiding his shaft home. I cried out at the deepness, my ass circling the delicious fullness stretching me as I settled onto him. "That's it, beautiful. »

Strong arms coiled around my torso, his warm palms flattening against my shoulder blades. He cradled me to him as he began to roll his groin against me. I clutched his chest for leverage as he sought the perfect angle. He shifted, the friction of his movement urging my seam wider so that my clit raked across the coarse patch of hair at his root. My head tipped forward, and I barely noticed the smart of pain as my forehead pressed into his shoulder.

"I want to be inside of you every day for the rest of my life. I wish I was strong enough to give you up, but I'm not," he said gruffly into my ear.

"You promised me forever," I whimpered, as my hips sought to drive him deeper inside me. There was no escape. I wouldn't allow it.

"And I'll give it to you. Forever," he repeated, plunging harder until I was nearly bouncing. His arm dropped from my back, and he took my hand, pressing my palm to the center of his chest. "Yours. All of me. It's all yours. My future. My heart. My very life."

I closed my eyes and concentrated on his rapid, but

constant, heartbeat. My own life hadn't begun until the day I met him, and someday when he was gone, it would draw to a close. I'd spend every moment until then fighting for him.

We'd made a decision together, and we'd said a vow. But now we had faced that which would attempt to rip us apart, and we were still here.

"I love you, Smith Price." My mouth closed over his, skimming his lips lightly.

His groin constricted beneath me, and we rode toward our forever together, sharing soft kisses as we fought to get closer, preparing for the battle we faced outside these walls. When he finally slowed, his mouth curved into a cocky grin.

"You look pleased with yourself," I noted, even as I sagged against him. He had a right to look pleased. On the list of the world's top orgasms, that one had blown them all away.

"I was just thinking that I love you, Belle Price."

I tilted my head back to scowl playfully at him, even as a happy peacefulness descended over me.

"You should have objected before you said *I do*, beautiful." His index finger tipped my chin up, and he placed a cautious kiss on my bruised lips.

"Can I file some type of negotiated contract?" The truth was that I wanted his name as much as I wanted him. My own surname held nothing but sad memories. It was my father's name, not mine, and if I had to choose a man's name, Smith's was the one I wanted.

"I doubt your lawyer will advise that," he said dryly.

I huffed in mock exasperation. "Belle Price it is, I suppose."

"On that note"—he deposited me onto the bed and swung his legs over the side—"I'll be right back."

I slumped against the pillows, languid contentment taking residence in my limbs. I was blinking sleepily by the time he returned.

"I took the liberty of stealing this from your purse." He slipped back into bed, my wedding band pinched between his thumb and forefinger. "Because it belongs with you."

Smith captured my hand and gently urged the ring onto my finger. I stared at it, trying to process how much my feelings had evolved about wearing it. The circle of flawless diamonds set into gold no longer felt heavy. It no longer dazzled. It simply felt right. It was as timeless as our love. No beginning. No end. Just forever.

"If you'd prefer a different one…" he began.

But I shook my head and leaned forward to kiss him hard on the mouth. I blanched as my cheek bumped his accidentally, but I swallowed down the pain before he could spot it. "Don't you dare try to take this ring off my finger."

"Good, you can pick out my ring." He slid an arm around my back, and we lay there staring at the new addition to my finger.

I glanced at him in surprise.

"What?" He shrugged. "I belong to you, beautiful. If you don't want me to—"

"Oh, you are wearing one," I informed him.

"I like it when you're jealous," he teased, knitting our fingers together.

"I just want everyone to know you're mine," I whispered, "so they know how lucky I am."

"That makes two of us. Now get some rest, Mrs. Price," he ordered, tugging the covers over me.

"What about Ms. Price?" I countered.

"As long as you're a Price," he murmured as he reached up to dim the lights.

"Forever." My eyes closed as I fell into a dreamless sleep.

# CHAPTER TWENTY-FIVE

*P*urple. It was the only word filtering through the haze of painkillers clouding my brain. I lifted my hand and gingerly touched my swollen cheek. The woman in the mirror flinched as pain shot through me. No wonder Smith had been so hesitant to touch me. I looked like hell. No amount of makeup was covering this up, and trying to smooth foundation over the bruise seemed like a pretty bad idea.

Smith appeared behind me, watching my reaction in the mirror. His strong hands gripped my upper arms, and I closed my eyes, savoring the touch.

"Give it time," he commanded in a low voice. "I'm going to arrange for a nurse to stay with you today."

I spun around, shaking my head. "No, don't do that."

The thought of being alone with a stranger was too much to bear.

"I can't leave you like this, beautiful." He raised a hand to brush back my hair, taking care to avoid my wounds. I saw the horror in his eyes and, behind it, an emotion that stole my breath.

"Then don't leave me." I bit my lip in an attempt at seduction and immediately regretted it as a searing throb rocketed through my temple.

Smith reacted instantly in concern, but I pushed him away. I couldn't stomach his pity any more than I could the reality of what had happened. The police had found my car, but not the man who had attacked me. That fact, combined with the soporific effects of my pain medicine, had my emotions at maximum capacity.

I swallowed against the tears that seemed perpetually lodged in my throat. "I'll call my aunt."

"Are you sure?" Smith's eyes softened, as if to remind me that the fury he couldn't hide was in no way directed at me.

"Yes."

He waited while I made the call from the hotel phone, perhaps suspecting I hadn't planned to at all. When I hung up with Jane, he brushed a kiss over my lips.

"I love you."

I caught his hand, clutching it desperately.

"I'm coming back." He spoke solemnly, and I relaxed my hold, allowing him to gently pull away.

I wanted to tell him not to go. Or ask when he was returning. But some part of me that hadn't been shattered in yesterday's attack resisted. I wasn't that girl. I didn't want to be. I couldn't permit it to change me.

As soon as he was gone, I took another pain pill, swallowing it down with a gulp of wine. If I was going to spend all day pent up in a hotel room, I didn't want the option of thinking.

But even as a languid stupor descended over me, my brain continued to reel, replaying the attack on a constant loop. Smith hadn't told me that I had been targeted, a decision I saw as calculated. However, I knew it had been. Coincidence was bumping into a friend at a restaurant. Being beat up when your husband worked for the city's resident crime syndicate wasn't.

I froze when I heard a knock at the door and braced myself for Jane's reaction. If she had thought it strange that I'd given her the room number of a hotel, she hadn't said anything. But she wasn't anticipating this. I took a peek before I opened the door.

Jane's mouth went slack, and I had to drag her inside, locking the door swiftly behind us.

"Who did this?" she demanded, her voice thundering through the quiet room.

"My car was stolen." There was so much more to the story than that, but I wasn't certain I had the strength to tell it.

And then the questions began. Had the person been caught? Why was I at a hotel? Where was this boyfriend of mine anyway?

"He went out to handle things," I said, hoping the answer implied he was doing something simple like checking in with the police.

Jane guided me to the sofa and sat me down, worry creasing the lines on her elegant face. "Belle, are you in trouble? Is this is something else?"

I clenched my eyes shut, but it couldn't stop my tears. "I can't talk about it."

"Did he do this?" she asked in a low voice that sounded positively homicidal.

"No," I said firmly.

"But he knows who did." She didn't wait for my response before she was picking up her purse. "I'm taking you home."

"No!" I leapt up. I couldn't imagine what would happen if Smith returned to find me gone. I was already sick over whatever had drawn him away from here this morning. If I disappeared, he would go straight to Hammond.

"What are you hiding from?"

Everyone. No one. I didn't know how to answer.

"I'm safe here." That's all she needed to know.

"And Smith?"

"He's dealing with it." I couldn't tell her more than that, not while everything was so screwed up. I already wished I hadn't asked her to come. Too many people in my life were already caught up in this nightmare.

Jane's gaze drifted to my hand. Her mouth pressed into a thin line but she didn't say anything about the band of diamonds sparkling on my ring finger.

Another thing I would have to explain when the time was right. For now I was grateful that she seemed keen to ignore it.

I patted the spot next to me, and Jane sank back down, still holding her purse. A large manila envelope stuck out of the top of it.

"What's that?" I asked, eying it as my blood turned to ice.

"Nothing." She twisted the bag away from me, but I reached out and snatched it.

It was addressed to me. Tearing it open despite her protests, I withdrew a stack of legal documents. If I had thought things couldn't get any worse, I was wrong. I scanned through them, not understanding half of what they said but getting the gist.

My mother was moving forward with the legal action she'd threatened, and she'd made her case not only against me but also against my ownership stake in Bless. I stared at them for a long minute, saying nothing, and then I began to laugh. It racked my body, making my face throb, but I couldn't stop.

Jane yanked them out of my hand and studied them for a moment before tossing them across the room.

"Sod her," she announced, taking my hand.

Gradually my laughter subsided as I faced the reality that confronted me. I was being attacked on all sides, and I didn't know which direction to start throwing punches.

# CHAPTER TWENTY-SIX

y fingers drummed impatiently against my mug. The coffee in it was cold and had been for at least half an hour. I'd left Belle at the hotel over an hour ago. Withdrawing my mobile, I checked her message again. I was in the right place at the right time, but there was no Georgia. The longer I waited, the more exposed I made myself. I took out my wallet and tossed a few pounds on the table for wasting the waiter's time.

I wanted to believe she had forgotten, but as I started the Bugatti, my thoughts turned to more sinister explanations. Without thinking, I began to cut through traffic, heading back to a place where I'd vowed never to return. I arrived in record time, mostly due to breaking the speed limit at every opportunity. The street was deserted, which wasn't unusual given the time of day. Only the most hardcore of Velvet's clientele would be here at this hour, I thought, which gave me no pleasure.

Punching in the security code, I entered the familiar corridor that led straight into a past I'd wanted to leave behind me. Sultry music drifted through the air, a relatively tasteful choice for once. As I entered, I found the space entirely empty save for Ariel, Velvet's newest and most faithful barmaid.

She looked up from the bottles she was arranging, her expression quickly shifting from casual interest to surprise.

"Is Georgia here?" I asked as I started toward her office.

"Nope." Ariel glanced around, as if to make sure before turning back to stare at me. "She called in for the week. Some excuse. Hammond arranged for a temporary manager."

"Is he here?"

She shook her head, to my relief. The last thing I needed was one of Hammond's errand boys rushing back to inform him of my presence.

"I'll admit I didn't expect to see you back here," Ariel said a bit too conversationally.

I paused, studying her for a moment. Her pink hair was gelled into a Mohawk, and unlike the last time we'd met, she was wearing a t-shirt and jeans. She wasn't actually here to tend bar, which meant Velvet wasn't open.

Velvet never closed.

I relaxed my face into a smile and slid onto a barstool. I could be charming when necessary, but it was a lot fucking harder when every impulse in my body wanted to leap over the counter and throttle her.

"What are you doing here anyway?" I asked, fingering the edge of a napkin. "This place is dead."

Her eyes darted over her shoulder, but she continued to pull liquor from the cabinets to replenish her stock. Finally she turned around, bracing her palms against the edge of the wood and shrugged. "Inventory. We had a busy weekend. I don't like to get caught unprepared."

"I can respect that. Neither do I." I kept my tone conversational, but there was no ignoring the threats hidden beneath our words.

Ariel's pierced lip curled up, and she leaned lower so that her t-shirt flapped open to reveal her tits. "Why? You interested in doing something else?"

This was why I'd discounted her before. It was obvious she was hot for what went on in the club. She'd practically begged me to do a scene the last time I'd come here. That she'd been treated to a display of my dominance only sealed her interest. Her voyeurism had blinded to me to her true intentions, but it had also undercut her purpose.

It was a dangerous thing taking on a job when you couldn't control your desires. It had always undermined Georgia's power. Ariel appeared to suffer from the same lack of self-restraint.

I undid my cufflink, tossing it on the bar, and rolled up one sleeve. Ariel's tongue darted between her lips as I repeated the action on the other side to reveal my forearms. It was my signature move. The one that I had become known for amongst those in the lifestyle. Her eyes hooded as I stood up and analyzed her.

She was lacking in every way. Too eager. Too fresh. She'd watched but she'd never participated. Hammond must have seen something in her that I was missing. But then again, he liked the malleable type—women he could mold into whatever his black soul desired.

Ariel fidgeted in front of me, her fingers twisting together under my penetrating gaze.

*That's right.* I might have lost my desire for anonymous submission, but I hadn't lost my touch. There had been a time when I could walk into this room, pick out any woman I saw, and she'd be on her knees. Ariel was about to prove I still had that ability.

"I assume that's an offer." I slid off my tie and popped my top collar button. But that was where I stopped. My body belonged to Belle, and this bitch wasn't getting anything more than a hand around her throat. "Serpent Room, now."

It was easy to slip into the role of Dom, a fact that I took little comfort in as I walked toward the aptly named private room. It had always been my least favorite due to its gaudy use of snakeskin leather as its primary decor, but it was where this snake belonged. Ariel entered behind me and I pointed up. She scurried to the center of the room, lifting her arms to the row of shackles that hung overhead.

This was going to be far too easy.

"Do you want me to undress?" she asked hopefully.

Fuck no.

"Did I tell you to speak?" I growled.

She fell silent, and I went to work binding her wrists to the inescapable restraints.

"This is what you wanted," I accused, circling around her. "So much so that you're willing to feed yourself to the wolf."

"Yes, Sir," she panted.

I slapped her. "You don't get to call me that."

Her eyes fell even as her legs wiggled apart.

*That isn't where this is going.* I kept the thought to myself as I rounded on her restrained body. Her breathing sped up as I took a step closer. But rather than stripping her, I wrapped my arm over her shoulder and closed my fingers around her neck.

"You're going to answer some questions now."

The effect of my words was immediate. Ariel jerked against the shackles, trying desperately to free herself.

"It's too late for that. You wanted to be dominated, and I'm going to do just that. You're going to tell me every fucking thing I want to know." I squeezed her throat to emphasize that I was the one in control.

"No!"

My grip tightened, cutting off her air supply. "You're new at this, aren't you? No need to answer. I can't believe Hammond trusted you to do this job. That's why you came to work here, isn't it?"

I loosened my hold on her, and she gulped for air but didn't speak.

"I don't think you understand," I snarled, sliding my hand up to her jaw and capturing it. I leaned into her, my mouth pressed close to her ear as she tried to writhe away from me. "Desperate men lose control. I'm not desperate, but you have no idea how far I'm willing to go for answers.

That was a simple question, so answer it. Did he send you here?"

"Yes," she bit out.

"That wasn't so hard, was it?" I seized her hair with my other hand. "Have you been feeding him information on Georgia?"

She didn't answer, and I jerked her head back, yanking her hair at the roots.

"Yes!" she screamed.

I held her there. Now we were getting somewhere.

"And me?"

This time she whimpered. "Yes."

"How did he know where to find my wife?" It was a foregone conclusion that he'd discovered the truth about Belle, and I didn't have any more time to waste on ferreting out the answers I needed. Not after the attack. It wasn't going to be an isolated incident, and I wanted to know his next move.

"He's tracking her," she answered in a soft voice.

"How?" I demanded, forcing myself to ignore the fear that stirred inside me.

"Your mobiles. It was harder for him to get to your wife's, but then the stupid bitch left it in her office and went out to lunch. He's tracking all of you." She laughed at this, and I froze. I wanted to strangle her. I wanted her to gasp for her last breath, but I wasn't through with her yet.

"Georgia?" I asked.

"That's been taken care of."

I threw her head forward, ignoring her as she called after me. She deserved to die, but when Hammond realized she had betrayed him, he'd take care of that. I'd been finished doing his dirty work for too long to take care of her now.

Belle was safe for the moment. I'd made certain her mobile had made it home with the rest of her personal belongings before we left the hospital. But Georgia. I dialed her mobile again, but it went to voicemail.

"How would he do it?" I muttered to myself, leaving Velvet behind. The image of my father floating lifelessly in the pool swam to mind. His death had been ruled an accident.

*It's unfortunate what can happen when one's left alone.*

That's what Hammond had said to my mother at the funeral.

I didn't think, I just reacted. Georgia's flat was around the corner, and I didn't bother to look as I threw the Bugatti into drive and sped toward it.

An eerie silence greeted me as I entered her flat. She hadn't changed the locks in years, which was convenient for me but deadly for her. I flipped on the lights and began to search. Rushing into her bedroom, I caught sight of something just beyond the bed.

A hand.

I rounded the bed and dropped to my knees beside her into a pool of blood. Her eyelids fluttered as my hands went to the wound in her abdomen. There was too much blood. It spurted past my palms as I tried to apply pressure. She was pale even in the darkness, her lips turning a sickly shade of blue.

"Smith?" Her voice was faint—confused—as she fought to open her eyes.

"It's okay." But it wasn't. I let go of her and pulled my mobile out of my pocket. It slipped from my bloody hands, and I fumbled to retrieve it. Dialing 9-9-9, I yanked a sheet from her bed and wound it into a tight ball. Holding it to her wounds, I pulled her body with my free arm into my lap. Her dark hair pooled around her.

"He knows." Crimson spilled from her lips as her words bubbled out.

"I know. Hold on. Help is coming." I needed her to stay awake, but I was afraid to allow her to continue talking.

She tried to shake her head but lacked the strength. "He knows where she is."

"She's safe," I said as I shushed her. "She isn't at home."

"Smith!" Georgia swallowed against the frothy blood that came with the exclamation. "The man who came here..." She gasped, her face screwing up as she searched for her voice through the pain. "He made a call. He's going to the Westminster Royal."

The world stopped around me, realization colliding with horror. I had no idea how he had found her. No idea how long he had known. No idea what I would discover when I reached her. Fear seized my chest in an icy grip. I looked down at Georgia and whispered, "I'm sorry."

There was no choice between staying and going. No choice between these two women who occupied such vastly different corners of my life. One was my past. The other my future. And yet I was tethered to this spot.

"Go." Georgia's command was no more than a breathy

whisper, but I felt the thread tying us to one another snap. This had been our choice all along—a sacrifice we were both willing to make to be free.

I left her there, her life seeping out onto the carpet, knowing soon she would finally be liberated.

# CHAPTER TWENTY-SEVEN

*T*he Bugatti roared as I pushed the gas pedal to the floorboard, dodging in and out of traffic in a desperate attempt to get on the A3212. I kept my thoughts focused on the road. Turn. Merge. Being present was the only thing that kept me from drowning in my past or fearing for my future.

A car veered across the motorway, narrowly missing me as it tried to avoid the scene of an accident. I slammed on my brakes as the cars in front of me slowed to allow emergency crews to reach the scene.

I hit the steering wheel. "*This* is a fucking emergency!"

Reality screeched toward me as I came to a full stop. In gridlock there was no way to keep my thoughts from drifting to what had just happened. And the reality of the situation came to life in front of me.

Georgia's blood.

It was smeared over the wheel. On my hands. I rubbed

the wheel with my sleeve, but there was no way to wipe my hands.

It had been a sick joke for years: calling her my sister. A jibe we were all too fond of hurling at one another. But as a lump formed in my throat, I knew she was the closest thing I'd had to living family for most of my life. I had spent that time questioning her motives and being judgmental of her choices, but it was only now that I knew I had loved her. Maybe that was what it was like to have a sibling. Constant annoyance. Misunderstanding. Realizing what they meant to you far too late.

Hammond would answer for what he had done to her.

But the thought of her murder only made me more aware of the danger that Belle faced now.

Somehow, they knew where she was. It was entirely likely that they'd been following me this whole time, but I couldn't be certain. Ariel said they were tracking our mobiles, which meant it didn't matter that I'd left hers at her flat when I'd had mine with me the whole time.

I dialed her number anyway and waited until it went to voicemail.

Hitting the voice activation button, I asked for the Westminster Royal.

"Price. The penthouse," I ordered as soon as the front desk answered.

"I'm sorry," a cheerful girl chirped. "We have a 'do not disturb' request for that guest."

"No shit," I snapped, "I placed that request. I'm trying to reach my wife. It's an emergency."

"I'm sorry, sir. I can take a message if—"

I hung up on her. Why the fuck had I put that "do not disturb" instruction up? Because I'd stupidly thought she was safe, and now there was no way to warn her. I could call the police, but I had no doubt that my response time was more efficient than theirs. I tried her number one more time. God, I wanted to scream at her voicemail message.

I threw my mobile onto the passenger seat when she didn't answer. I had just pulled off the motorway when it began to ring.

"Belle?" I answered in a clipped tone. "You need to get out of there."

"This isn't Belle." Hammond's familiar voice crawled under my skin "Although it looks as if you're on your way to see her now. I'm sure she'll appreciate a romantic surprise more than getting a call ahead of time. She doesn't expect you to return to the hotel for hours after all. I'm told newlyweds are particularly sentimental. Perhaps you should pick her up some mums on the way."

I didn't miss the reference to funeral flowers. "Hammond, when I get my hands on you—"

"What, Smith? What will you do to me? You have had the opportunity to take me out for months and yet you never take it. Your father. Margot. You never sought retribution then." He paused, and for a moment, I thought the call had dropped. "Of course, perhaps this foolish witch hunt you've gotten caught up with is your own petty attempt."

"It's over," I warned him. "You know who's been investigating you."

"Yes, I do," Hammond said, sounding nonplussed. "Albert was investigating me as well. I think he had about as much evidence as either you or his son do now."

"Why?" He wanted to brag, and I wanted to keep him talking. If he was on the line with me, he couldn't be hurting her. "Why go after Clara? Why Belle?"

"I suppose I'm a bit of a romantic. I love a tragic love story. Did Samantha tell you that when you visited her?"

My blood ran cold, and I gripped the wheel, my knuckles turning white. I could see Westminster Royal ahead, but it wasn't close enough. "You spoke to Samantha?"

"Of course. Do you honestly think she escaped to New York and started over? I really thought you were smarter than that. If I'd known you weren't, I wouldn't have bothered putting you through law school. Samantha is, shall we say, indebted to me. You can understand that."

I didn't care to hear more about Samantha's betrayal. Not when so much was on the line. "You haven't answered my question."

"Oh, yes, why prey on your sweet, young wives? Honestly, Clara was simply a means to an end. I wanted Albert out of the picture and, boy, was her ex-boyfriend a crackpot. After his own attempts failed, he was so grateful to have my help. He only wanted to keep her from Alexander. We had several opportunities really, but it was so poetic to have it happen at the wedding—and no one doubted for a minute why he'd done it. They assumed it was the efforts of a mad man, and the King simply got in the way. Nothing covers up one sin like another scandal."

"Alexander guessed. He knew there was more to it." I took pride in that now, in my fragile camaraderie with a man who had the ability to see through to the evil at the heart of such actions.

"Of course, he did, but that hardly mattered since he hesitated to make a move. Too much information. Who could he trust? He couldn't take action. But you knew that, didn't you? When you went to him and begged for him to finally see this thing through to the end. It was how I found out that you'd gotten married. That stung, son. I shouldn't have heard it from someone else."

"I'm not your son," I growled.

"I would have sent my congratulations earlier," he continued, ignoring me, "but I didn't have your current address. My present is being delivered now."

"If you touch one hair on her head—"

"I wouldn't dream of touching her. Belle is a lovely girl. Our mutual friend was quite put out that he didn't get to spend enough quality time with her the other evening."

"Stop this," I demanded. "You can have me. No struggle. I'll come to you. Alexander won't have me as a witness. Just leave her be."

"And call off Jake's fun? He's been looking forward to seeing you again. Give him my regards."

Then the line went dead.

# CHAPTER TWENTY-EIGHT

*I* sat up in bed, rubbing my eyes out of habit. White-hot pain pierced my temple. I blinked back the tears that flooded to my bruised eye. This was going to take some getting used to.

"How are you feeling?" Jane asked, her eyes crinkling in concern when I finally reached the parlor.

"Fine," I lied. I might feel better when Smith was back, and when I could finally leave here. I'd chosen sleep rather than obsessing over his return.

Jane got to her feet, examining me as she came closer. "Do you want another pain pill?"

I shook my head, but the sudden motion loosed a new wave of pain, and I flinched.

"I think you better have one, love."

I didn't put up a fight as she went for my prescription bottle and a glass of water.

"Have you eaten anything today?" she asked as I swallowed the pill.

"No," I admitted sheepishly. "I haven't really eaten anything since last night. My stomach is bothering me."

"Of course, it is." She frowned. "That's an opiate. You shouldn't take it on an empty stomach."

I sighed. As usual, she was probably right. "I guess we could order room service."

"Or there's that curry place around the corner?" she offered. "We could get some fresh air."

It was a calculated suggestion. Jane was still trying to suss out what was going on. I didn't want to tell her that Smith would lose his shit if he found out I'd left the hotel. Instead I pointed to my face. "I'm not quite ready to debut this in daylight hours."

"I suppose that makes sense." But there was doubt in her voice. "I'll only be a few minutes."

"I'll be fine." So far Jane had been more of a babysitter than a nurse. Sitting on the sofa while I napped and plying me with pain pills when I woke. And questioning me at every opportunity.

"Okay, it's just a jaunt. I almost forgot." She pulled my mobile out of her bag. "You left this at home. Best you have it."

"Thank you." Contact with the world outside seemed like a pretty novel concept at this point. I frowned when I saw a missed call from Smith. No doubt he was freaking out that I didn't answer.

"I'll be right back."

I locked the door behind Jane and immediately called him back, but the phone went to voicemail. Checking the time stamp, I realized he'd only called a few minutes before. He was probably already trying to call me again.

I tugged at my pajamas. They clung to me, sticky with the sweat of nightmares. A bath seemed like a pretty good idea. If Smith was going to have to encounter this mug when he got back, the rest of me could be presentable. It would be good to feel human again. Plus, I'd never gotten a chance to clean up after last night's lovemaking.

That was the trouble with all these meds. I couldn't quite function normally. They made me move in slow motion. I blinked, drowsily, as the latest dose began to take effect. For a second, I considered if it was smart to take a bath, but Jane would be back momentarily, and who ever drowned in a tub?

I opened the music app on my mobile and found my Rolling Stones playlist. Listening to the music Smith loved soothed me. I turned up the volume and dropped it on the unmade bed.

I turned the tap on, waiting for the water to get hot as I slipped out of my pajamas and into a hotel robe, then studied myself in the mirror. The bruise had begun to turn black, yellowing around the edges. Since there was nothing they could do about the hairline fraction other than wait, I was stuck with the swelling until it healed. Thank God I didn't have any business meetings scheduled.

I let my hair down, noting how far past my shoulders it already was. Maybe when my parole was up, I could see a stylist. I'd have to keep the fringe to hide the gruesome scar the stitches would leave.

*Focus on what you can change,* I told myself. I could deal with the scars left on my body, the rest would take time.

Walking over to the tub, I dipped my finger in to check the temperature.

Perfect. Relief was at hand.

My fingers closed over the knot of my robe, but before I could tug it loose, my ringtone interrupted the music.

Dashing back for it, I made it halfway across the room when a shape hurtled toward me. I barely had time to brace myself before I slammed into the wall. The ringtone ended, and my mobile began to play "Give Me Shelter."

Falling to the floor, I scrambled backwards, dragging myself by my hands toward the bathroom. I reached the door before the assailant did, kicking it shut with my foot. Jumping up, I turned the lock and searched the room frantically. The door shook on its hinges as the man bashed against it repeatedly.

I spotted a window above the toilet and ran for it. Balancing precariously on the toilet lid, I tried to pry the window open. It was nailed shut. Looking around, I grabbed a towel, wrapped it around my hand and ducked as I put my first through the glass. It shattered, shards skimming across my face and clattering to the floor. I pushed aside the remaining glass with the towel and pulled myself up. I stuck my head out, noting with dismay that it was almost a dead drop from the eighth floor. But there was a small ledge below that felt a whole lot safer than sticking around here. I wriggled farther through the opening, catching my shoulder on a large shard. It sliced through my skin, but I barely felt it.

And then I heard the door fly open. I moved faster, deciding then and there that I'd rather fall to my fate than stay here to be murdered. I had my hips nearly out of the window when hands closed over my ankles. I screamed as loudly as I could, hoping it would carry over the traffic to the tourists below.

He hauled me back inside, slamming me to the tile and kicking me hard in the ribs. I curled into a ball. There didn't seem to be any other option but to take it and hope.

"Miss me?" he asked, and I froze at the familiar voice.

"Our date ended so suddenly the other night. I tried to call and apologize, but you haven't been answering your phone, Belle. So I thought I'd stop by and see how you're doing." He jerked me up by the hair, dragging me to my feet to face him. I hadn't seen much of him in the dark, but I saw now that he was about Smith's age. Good-looking. Except for the homicidal mania glinting in his eyes.

"Wow, that is beautiful." He gripped my face roughly and I screamed. A wicked smirk twitched on his lips. "Do you mind if I take a picture of my handiwork? I so rarely get a good before shot. There's a really lovely sense of movement when someone's still alive. It's just not the same after I've already killed them."

I said the only word that came to mind. "Please."

"Please?" he laughed. "Do you have any idea the man you married or what he's capable of? Sorry, baby, this is eye for an eye. I'd love for you to tell him hello, but unfortunately, you'll be in no condition to deliver the message."

He dropped his hold on my face, curled his fist and punched me in the stomach. My mouth gaped, searching for air. I was still gasping when he shoved me into the bathtub. Fluid shot down my throat, burning my lungs. My hands flew wildly, splashing against the porcelain, searching for a grip.

And then he let me go.

# CHAPTER TWENTY-NINE

*T*he Rolling Stones greeted me as I walked into the suite. I called Belle's name but all I heard was a violent splash. I skidded into the bathroom as Jake plunged her face back into the water, holding her head under. I raced toward him, springing mid-step and tackling him. Belle arched out of the tub, spluttering as she collapsed to the floor.

"Go!" I yelled just as Jake knocked me off my feet.

Metal glinted as he lunged toward me, and my hand shot out, catching his wrist. We struggled as Belle shook a few yards from us, still trying to catch her breath.

Christ, she might need CPR, and I was in no position to give it.

I swung my knees up, managing to catch him in the ribs and throw him to the side. I rolled on top of him, forcing his wrist and the knife over his head.

"You son of a bitch," I spit at him.

"You knew this was coming, Price." He struggled to

speak as we both fought to keep the knife in our control. "You've known for years."

"I had nothing to do with her death." But it didn't matter what I told him, and I was well past willing to negotiate with this piece of shit.

"Margot would be here now—"

"If it weren't for Hammond," I screamed. "How do you still not understand that?"

Of course Hammond had chosen him for this. A man with a vendetta was harder to fight. Good thing I had one of my own.

"She was going to leave you," he panted under me, "and you couldn't take it. Couldn't admit that she didn't love you."

"I don't care who she was fucking. We were both fucking anything that moved. She was still my wife. I would never have hurt her."

"Even though she was going to expose you for what you really were and take all your money?"

Glass ground into the tile as I heard Belle's palms sliding over the floor, but to my horror, she sounded as if she was coming closer instead of running.

Jake smiled, his eyes darting over my shoulder. "And now I'm going to take her away from you. That's what you deserve."

I took a deep breath, braced myself and head-butted him. His nose crunched on impact, but I shook off the momentary daze.

Jake lolled back, stunned, which gave me enough time

to snatch away the knife. I backed away from him slowly as I got to my feet, keeping the weapon in front of me.

"Are you okay, beautiful?" I called, not daring to take my eyes off Jake. He'd clamped his hand over his nose, but he wasn't down for the count.

"I'm fine," she answered in a breathless voice.

"I want you to go. Walk out of here and go down to the front desk. Tell them to call the police."

"I'm not leaving you here," she cried.

"For once, do as I say," I ordered. We were nowhere near out of danger and wouldn't be until I got her out of this room. Then I could take care of this once and for all.

"Have you told her?" Jake asked with bloodstained teeth. "About your first wife?"

"I know," Belle called petulantly over my shoulder.

"Then you know why this is going to happen. If I don't do it, someone else will. We live by a code. Eye for an eye. Retribution."

"How biblical of you," she shot back.

How was it possible that I could love her and want to strangle her at the same time? I shot a warning glare over my shoulder.

"Go," I repeated in a low voice.

"Not a chance."

"You seem like a nice girl. Spirited," Jake called as he struggled to his feet. Abandoning his bloody nose, he began to brush glass off his clothes. "I think Margot would have liked her. What do you think, Price?"

"Don't move," I warned him.

"I bet she's wild, too. Let's have a little fun for old times' sake. You can watch. She was so hot for it the other night, but I bet you already knew that." Jake took a step closer. "Did you forget how to share? We always shared. That's the problem with adults. We forget our manners. What did you say the first time you shared Margot? 'Careful, she bites.' Christ, you had to ride that bitch from behind if you didn't want stitches."

Belle inhaled sharply at this revelation.

"That was a long time ago, Jake. We were kids, just like you said, and I grew up." I said it more for her benefit than his.

"It's a pity. It seems like you grew up when you cut those brake lines in her car. That was a very selfish thing to do."

"I had nothing to do with that." I didn't know why we were still arguing, except that I hadn't gotten Belle out of the suite yet.

"I've been thinking. Since you're going to get to see Margot first, give her my love. Although I doubt she's hanging around saving you a seat. But then there's a special spot in hell for you."

Suddenly, he ran at me. My hand lashed out, knocking Belle toward the wall seconds before he launched into me. We stumbled backwards, flipping over and landing in a heap at the foot of the bed. Jake didn't move. Pushing his body off me, he fell over, the knife sticking out of his chest.

Belle clawed against the doorframe, rising, eyes wide with horror as she took in the scene.

"Come here," I said softly.

She looked apprehensively at his body, still clinging to

the door. I forced myself to stand, ignoring the sharp pinch in my side as I went to her.

"Oh my God." She clapped a hand over her mouth as she took in my blood-stained clothes.

"Not mine," I reassured her. She'd been in no condition to realize they were bloodied when I arrived, and right now I didn't have the time to explain. "I need you to leave. Go to Alexander and Clara. You'll be safe with them."

As safe as she would be anywhere.

She shook her head frantically. "I won't leave you."

"Don't be stubborn. For once, I'm *not* in the mood to be provoked." I forced a smile. "Go and call the police from the front desk and then call Clara."

She looked to the mobile still playing music on the bed.

"Don't use that one," I said in a flat voice. "You have their numbers?"

She nodded. "Smith...you need a witness."

"They'll take me in for questioning, beautiful. It's clearly a case of self-defense." Tears pooled in her eyes, but I took her hand. "I'm a lawyer, remember?"

"I don't want to leave you," she whispered.

"I know." I brushed a kiss over her lips. "But we both know that's not Hammond lying there. I need to know you're safe. As soon as they release me, I'll come to you."

She didn't question that logic, even though she was smart enough to know I wouldn't be joining her any time soon.

"I love you," she said softly.

"I love you, too." I trailed a finger down her throat long-ingly. "Birds of a feather, right? You're a helluva fighter."

"I'll fight for you," she promised.

I closed my eyes and pushed her away, the implication clear. She kept a hold of my hand, and I heard a choked sob as our fingers slipped apart. Then she was gone.

I dropped to the floor, holding my side. I pulled out my mobile and dialed a number from memory. "I want to report a murder."

## ACKNOWLEDGMENTS

Thank you to super agent Mollie Glick for supporting what I want to write, and to Joy Fowlkes who keeps things running smoothly. My foreign agent, Jessica Regal, is a goddess. I can't wait to see all my dirty words in other languages.

Lindsey, you keep my life functioning, and you were doing that long before you became my assistant. Yep, I'm cribbing this from last time because it's still true. I'm sorry for making your life hell!

Elise, I hope I didn't make you blush too hard. Thank you for all the hard work you've put in on things while I'm on deadline. Here's to many more releases.

A huge thanks to Sharon, who is the best publicist I've ever had! You're a genius and not just because we think alike! And all my love and thanks to the Sassy Savvy Fabulous team—Linda, Jesey, and Melissa. You rock my publicity and marketing world!

Thank you to Bethany and Josh for impeccable editorial

services available at the last minute. Somehow you always know what I mean to say, even when I don't. And thanks to Cait Greer for putting up with all my formatting needs.

I get by with a little help from my friends and significant amounts of booze.Thanks Laurelin, Sierra, Melanie, Tamara, and Kayti for always being there.

To the FYW girls, you have owned this year, and I'm so lucky to get to be a (small) part of that.

A big thank you to the ladies of the Royal Court! You make me want to get up every morning.

Thank you to all the bloggers who've shown such enthusiasm and love for the series. You've made a huge difference in my life.

I had the amazing pleasure of attending a writer's retreat while I was working on this novel. I'm so blessed to count Amy Jackson, Michelle Leighton, Addison Moore, Samantha Young, Chelsea Fine, Michelle A. Valentine, Amy Bartol, Raine Miller, and Janet Wallace as members of my tribe. Thank you for not letting me work to hard. Next year in Palm Springs?

I wouldn't be doing this if not for the support of my family. Thanks, kids, for cheering on my books even if I won't let you read them yet, and to my husband, who lets me spend time with the men in my head without getting (too) jealous. Love you.

# ABOUT THE AUTHOR

Geneva Lee is the *New York Times, USA Today*, and internationally bestselling author of over a dozen novels. Her bestselling Royals Saga has sold over one million copies worldwide. She is the co-owner of Away With Words, a destination bookstore in Poulsbo, Washington. When she isn't traveling, she can usually be found writing, reading, or buying another pair of shoes.

*Learn more about Geneva Lee at:*
www.GenevaLee.com